Honeycomb
Pilgrimage
Vol. 3

by

Dorothy M. Richardson

Double 9
BOOKS

Honeycomb
Pilgrimage
Vol. 3
by Dorothy M. Richardson

ISBN: 978-93-61159-22-0

Published by

DOUBLE 9 BOOKS

2/13-B, Ansari Road
Daryaganj, New Delhi ¬ 110002
info@double9books.com
www.double9books.com
Tel. 011-40042856

ABOUT THE AUTHOR

At the outbreak of World War I, he joined the Royal Flying Corps and worked as an assistant to David Henderson and Hugh Trenchard in France. Throughout the war, he wrote with Lady Juliet Duff, the widow of Sir Robin Duff, 2nd Baronet of Vaynol, who was killed on October 16, 1914, near Oostnieuwekirke while fighting in the 2nd Life Guards. The letters were ultimately published under the title Dear Animated Bust: Letters to Lady Juliet Duff. Richardson was born in Abingdon in 1873, as the third of four daughters. After the fourth daughter was born, Dorothy's father (Charles) began referring to her as his son. Richardson, meantime, "also attributed this habit to her own boylike willfulness". She lived at 'Whitefield', a huge mansion-style residence on Albert Park erected by her father in 1871 and currently owned by Abingdon School. Her family relocated to Worthing, West Sussex, in 1880, and then to Putney, London, in 1883. During her time in London, she "attended a progressive school influenced by the ideas of John Ruskin", in which "the pupils were encouraged to think for themselves". in which she "studied French, German, literature, logic and psychology".

CONTENTS

CHAPTER I

1

When Miriam got out of the train into the darkness she knew that there were woods all about her. The moist air was rich with the smell of trees — wet bark and branches — moss and lichen, damp dead leaves. She stood on the dark platform snuffing the rich air. It was the end of her journey. Anything that might follow would be unreal compared to that moment. Little bulbs of yellow light further up the platform told her where she must turn to find the things she must go to meet. "How lovely the air is here." ... The phrase repeated itself again and again, going with her up the platform towards the group of lights. It was all she could summon to meet the new situation. It satisfied her; it made her happy. It was enough; but no one would think it was enough.

But the house was two miles off. She was safe for the present. Throughout the journey from London the two-mile drive from the station had stood between her and the house. The journey was a long solitary adventure; endless; shielded from thoughts of the new life ahead and leaving the past winter in the Gunnersbury villa far away; vanquished, almost forgotten. She could only recall the hours she had spent shivering apathetically over small fires; a moment when she had brought a flush of tears to her mother's eyes by suddenly telling her she was maddeningly unreasonable, and another moment alone with her father when she had stood in the middle of the hearth-rug with her hands behind her and ordered him to abstain from argument with her in the presence of her mother — "because it gives her pain when I have to show you that I am at least as right as you are" — and he had stood cowed and silent.... Then the moment of accepting the new post, the last days of fear and isolation and helplessness in hard winter weather and the setting off in the main line train that had carried her away from everything — into the spring. Sitting in the shabbily upholstered unexpectedly warm and comfortable main line train she had seen through the mild muggy air bare woods on the horizon, warm and tawny, and on the near copses a ruddy purpling bloom. Surprise had kept her thoughtless and rapt. Spring — a sudden pang of tender green seen in suburban roadways in

April ... one day in the Easter holidays, bringing back the forgotten summer and showing you the whole picture of summer and autumn in one moment ... but evidently there was another spring, much more real and wonderful that she had not known—not a clear green thing, surprising and somehow disappointing you, giving you one moment and then rushing your thoughts on through vistas of leafage, but tawny and purple gleamings through soft mist, promising ... a vision of spring in dim rich faint colours, with the noisy real rushing spring still to come ... a thing you could look at and forget; go back into winter, and see again and again, something to remember when the green spring came, and to think of in the autumn ... spring; coming; perhaps spring was coming all the year round.... She looked back, wondering. This was not the first time that she had been in the country in March. Two years ago, when she had first gone out into the world it had been March ... the night journey from Barnes to London, and on down to Harwich, the crossing in a snowstorm, the afternoon journey across Holland—grey sky, flat bright green fields, long rows of skeleton poplars. But it was dark before they reached the wooded German country—the spring must have been there, in the darkness. And now coming to Newlands she had seen it. The awful blind cold effort of coming to Newlands had brought a new month of spring; there for always.... And this was the actual breath of it; here, going through her in the darkness.... Someone was at her side, murmuring her name, a footman. She moved with him towards a near patch of light which they reached without going through the station building, and in a moment the door of a little brougham closed upon her with a soft thud. She sat in the softly lit interior, holding her umbrella and her undelivered railway ticket in careful fingers. The footman and a porter were hoisting her Saratoga trunk. Their movements sounded muffled and far-off. The brougham bowled away through the darkness softly. The lights of the station flickered by and disappeared. The brougham windows were black. No sound but the faint rumble of the wheels along the smooth road. Miriam relaxed and sat back, smiling. For a moment she was conscious of nothing but the soft-toned, softly lit interior, the softness at her back, the warmth under her feet and her happy smile; then she felt a sudden strength; the smile coming straight up so unexpectedly from some deep where it had been waiting, was new and strong and exhilarating. It would not allow itself to dimple; it carried her forward, tiding her over the passage into new experience and held her back, at the same time; it lifted her and held her suspended over the new circumstances in rapid contemplation. She pressed back more steadily into the elastic softness and sat with bent head, eagerly watching her thoughts ... this is me; this is right; I'm *used* to dainty broughams; I can take everything for granted.... I must take everything absolutely for granted.... The moments passed, carrying her rapidly on. There was a life ahead that was going to enrich and change her as she had been enriched and changed by Hanover, but much more swiftly and intimately. She was changed already. Poverty and discomfort had been shut out of her life when the brougham door closed upon her. For as long as she could endure and achieve any sort of dealing with the new situation, they had gone, the worry and pain of them could not touch her. Things that rose warm and laughing and expanding within her now, that had risen to the beauty and music and happiness of Germany and been crushed because she was the despised pupil teacher, that had dried up and seemed to die in the English boarding school, were going to be met and satisfied ... she looked down at the hands clasped on her knees, the same hands and knees that had ached with cold through long winter days in the basement schoolroom ... chilblains ... the everlasting unforgettable aching of her sore throat ... things that had made her face yellow and stiff or flushed with fever ... gone away for ever. Her old self had gone, her governess self. It had really gone weeks ago, got up and left her in that moment when she had read Mrs. Corrie's letter in Bennett's villa in the middle of a bleak February afternoon. A voice had seemed to come from the large handwriting scrawling across the faint blue page under the thick neat small address in raised gilt. The same voice, begging her to come for a few weeks and try seemed to resound gently in the brougham. She had not accepted the situation; she had accepted something in Mrs. Corrie's imagined voice coming to her confidently from the big wealthy house.

The brougham passed a lamp and swerved in through a gate, bowling along over softly crunching gravel. She pressed reluctantly against the cushioned back. The drive had been too short.... Bennett's friends had given the Corries wrong ideas about her. They wanted a governess. She was not a governess. There were governesses ... the kind of person they wanted. It was a mistake; another mistake ... the brougham made a beautiful dull humming, going along a tree-lined tunnel.... What did the Corries want of her, arriving in their brougham? What did they expect her to do?...

2

As the footman opened the door of the brougham, a door far back in the dim porch was flung back, letting out a flood of light, and the swift figure of a parlourmaid who seized Miriam's Gladstone bag and the silver-mounted Banbury Park umbrella and led the way across the porch into the soft golden blaze. The Saratoga trunk had gone away with the brougham, and in a moment the door was closed and Miriam was standing, frightened and alone, in a fire-lit, lamp-lit, thickly carpeted enclosure within sound of a thin chalky voice saying "Ello, ello." It seemed to come from above her. "Ello—ello—ello—ello," it said busily, hurrying about somewhere above as she gazed about the terrifying hall. It was somehow like the box office of a large theatre, only much better; the lamplight, there seemed to be several lamps shaded with low-hanging old gold silk, and the rosy light from the huge clear fire in a deep grate fell upon a thick pale greeny yellow carpet, the little settees with their huge cushions, and the strange-looking pictures set low on dull gold walls. In two directions the hall went dimly away towards low archways screened by silently hanging bead curtains. "Ello—ello—ello—ello," said the voice coming quickly downstairs. Half raising her eyes Miriam saw a pale turquoise blue silk dress, long and slender with deep frills of black chiffon round the short sleeves and a large frill draping the low-cut bodice, a head and face, sheeny bronze and dead white, coming across the hall.

"Ow-de-do; so glad you've come," said the voice, and two thin fingers and a small thin crushed handkerchief were pressed against her half-raised hand.

"Are you famished? Deadly awful journey! I'm glad you're tall. Wiggerson'll take up your things. You must be starvin'. Don't change. There's only me. Don't be long. I shall tell them to put on the soup."

Gently propelled towards the staircase Miriam went mechanically up the wide shallow stairs towards the parlourmaid waiting at the top. Behind her she heard the swift fuffle of Mrs. Corrie's dress, the swish of a bead curtain and the thin tuneless voice inaccurately humming in some large near room, "Jack's the boy for work; Jack's the boy for play." She followed the maid across the landing, walking swiftly, as Mrs. Corrie had done—the same greeny carpet, but white walls up here and again strange pictures hung low, on a level with your eyes, strange soft tones ... crayons? ... pastels?—what was the word—she was going to live with them, she would be able to look at them—and everything up here, in the soft pink light. There were large lamps with rose-pink shades. The maid held back a pink silk curtain hanging across an alcove, and Miriam went through to the open door of her room. "Harris will bring up your trunk later, miss—if you like to leave your keys with me," said the maid behind her. "Oh yes," said Miriam carelessly, going on into the room. "Oh, I don't know where they are. Oh, it doesn't matter, I'll manage."

"Very good, miss," said Wiggerson politely, and came forward to close the bedroom door.

Miriam flung off her outer things and faced herself in the mirror in her plain black hopsack dress with the apple green velveteen pipings about the tight bodice and the square box sleeves which filled the square mirror from side to side as she stood. "This dress is a nightmare in this room," she thought, puffing up her hair under her fringe-net with a hat-pin. "Never mind, I mustn't think about it," she added hurriedly, disconcerted for a moment by the frightened look in her eyes. The distant soft flat silvery swell of a little gong sent her hurrying to the mound of soft bath towel in the wide pale blue wash-hand basin. She found a bulging copper hot-water jug, brilliantly polished, with a wicker-covered handle. The water hissed gently into the wide shallow basin, sending up a great cloud of comforting steam. Dare's soap ... extraordinary. People like this being taken in by advertisements ... awful stuff, full of free soda, *any* transparent soap is bad for the skin, must be, in the nature of things ... makes your skin feel tight. Perhaps they only use it for their hands.... Advertisement will do anything, Pater said.... Perhaps in houses like this—plonk, it certainly made a lovely hard ring falling into the basin—where everything was warm and clean and fragrant even Dare's soap could not hurt you. The room behind her seemed to encourage the idea. But surely it couldn't be her room. It was a spare room. They had put her into it for her month on trial. Could it possibly be hers, just her room, if she stayed ... the strange, beautiful, beautiful long wide hang of the faintly patterny faintly blue curtains covering the whole of the window space; the firelight on them as she came into the room with Wiggerson, the table with a blotter, there had been a table by the door with a blotter, as Wiggerson spoke. She looked round, there it was ... the blue covered bed, the frilled pillows, high silky-looking bed curtains with some sort of little pattern on them, the huge clear fire, the big wicker chair.

3

Miriam laughed over her strange hot wine-clear wine-flavoured soup ... *two* things about soup besides taking it from the side of your spoon, which everybody knows—you *eat* soup, and you tilt your plate *away*, not towards you (chum along, chum along and eat your nice hot soup).... Her secure, shy, contented laugh was all right as a response to Mrs. Corrie, sitting at the head of the long table, a tall graceful bird, thin broad shoulders, with the broad black frill slipping from them, rather broad thin oval white face, wiry auburn Princess of Wales fringe coming down into a peak with hollow beaten-in temples each side of it, auburn coils shining as she moved her head and the chalky lisping voice that said little things and laughed at them and went on without waiting for answers. But to herself the laugh meant much more than liking Mrs. Corrie and holding her up and begging her to go on. It meant the large dark room, the dark invisible picture, the big pieces of strange dark furniture in gloomy corners, the huge screen near the door where the parlourmaid came in and out; the table like an island under the dome of the low-hanging rose-shaded lamp, the table-centre thickly embroidered with beetles' wings, the little dishes stuck about, sweets, curiously crusted brown almonds, sheeny grey-green olives; the misty beaded glass of the finger bowls—Venetian glass from that shop in Regent Street—the four various wine glasses at each right hand, one on a high thin stem, curved and fluted like a shallow tulip, filled with hock; and floating in the warmth amongst all these things the strange, exciting, dry sweet fragrance coming from the mass of mimosa, a forest of little powdery blossoms, little stiff grey—the arms of railway signals at junctions—Japanese looking leaves—standing as if it were growing, in a shallow bowl under the rose-shaded lamp.

"Mélie's coming on Friday."

The parlourmaid set before Miriam a small shapely fish, with scales like mother-of-pearl and pink fins, lying in a curl of paper. "Red mullet," she exclaimed to herself; "how on earth do I know that it's red mullet? And those *are* olives, of course." Mrs. Corrie was humming to herself about Mélie as the fork in her thin little fingers plucked fitfully at the papered fish. "Do you know planchette?" she asked, in a faint singsong, turning with a little bold pounce to the salt-cellar close at Miriam's left hand. "Oh-h-h" said Miriam intelligently.... "Planchette ... Planchette ... Cloches de Corneville. Planquette. Is planchette a part of all this?... Planchette, a French dressmaker, perhaps." She turned fully round to Mrs. Corrie and waited, smiling sympathetically. "It's deadly uncanny," Mrs. Corrie went on, "I can tell you. *Deadly.*" Her delicate voice stopped fearfully and she glanced at Miriam with a laugh. "I don't believe I know what it is," said Miriam, sniffing in the scent of the mimosa and savouring the delicate flavour of the fish. These things would go on after planchette was disposed of, she thought, and took a sip of hock.

"It's deadly. I hope Mélie'll bring one. She's a fairy; real Devonshire fairy. She'll make it work. We'll have *such* fun."

"What is it?" said Miriam a little uneasily.... A fairy and a planchette and fun—silly laughter, some tiresome sort of game; a hoax.

"I tell you *all* about it, all, all ..." intoned Mrs. Corrie provisionally, whilst the maid handed the tiny ready-cut saddle of lamb. "Spinnich? Ah, nicey spinnich; you can leave us that, Stokes.... Oh, you *must* have Burgundy—spin-spin and Burgundy; awful good; a thimble-full, half a glass; that's right."

The clear dry hock had leapt to Miriam's brain and opened her eyes, the Burgundy spread through her limbs, a warm silky tide. The green flavour of the spinach, tasting of earth, and yet as smooth as cream intoxicated her. Surely nothing could so delicately build up your strength as these small stubby slices of meat so tender that it seemed to crumble under your teeth.... "It's an awful thing. It whirls about and writes with a pencil. Writes. All sorts of things," said Mrs. Corrie, with a little frightened laugh. "Really. No nonsense. Names. Anythin'. Whatever you're thinkin' about. It's uncanny, I can tell you."

"It sounds most extraordinary," said Miriam, with a firm touch of scepticism.

"You wait. Oh—you wait," sang Mrs. Corrie in a whisper. "I shall find out, I shall find out, if you're not careful, I shall find out his name."

Miriam blushed violently. "Ah-ha," beamed Mrs. Corrie in a soft high monotone. "*I* shall find out. We'll have *such* fun."

"Do you *believe* in it?" said Miriam, half irritably.

"You wait—you wait—you wait, young lady. Mélie'll be here on Friday day."

The rich caramel, the nuts and dessert, Mrs. Corrie's approval of her refusal of port wine with her nuts, the curious, half-drowsy chill which fell upon the table, darkening and sharpening everything in the room as the broken brown nutshells increased upon their trellis-edged plates were under the spell of the strange woman. Mrs. Corrie kept on talking about her; Mélie—born in Devonshire, seeing fairies, having second sight, being seen one day staring into space by a sportsman, a fisherman, a sort of poet, who married her and brought her to London. Did Mrs. Corrie really believe that she knew everything? "I believe she's a changeling," laughed Mrs. Corrie at last—"oh, it's cold. Chum-long, let's go."

4

"We can't go into my little room," said Mrs. Corrie, turning to Miriam with a little excited catch in her voice, as the bead curtain rattled gently into place behind them. "It's bein' re-done." Just ahead of them, beyond a mystery of palms to right and left, a door opened upon warm brilliance. Miriam heard the busy tranquil flickering of a fire. "I see," she said eagerly. "Why does she explain?" she wondered, as they passed into the large clear room. How light it was, fairyland, light and fragrant and very warm. The light was high; creamy bulbs, high up, and creamy colour everywhere, cream and gold stripes, stripy chairs of every shape, some of them with twisted gilt legs, curious oval pictures in soft half-tones, women in hats, strange groups, all tilted forward like mirrors.

"Ooogh—barracky, ain't it? I hate empty droin'-rooms," said Mrs. Corrie, sweeping swiftly about, pushing up great striped easy chairs towards the fire. Miriam stood in a dream, watching the little pale hands in the clear light, dead white fingers, rings, twinkling green and sea blue, and the thin cruel flash of tiny diamonds ... harpy hands ... dreadful and clever ... one of the hands came upon her own and compelled her to drop into a large cushioned chair.

"Like him black?" came the gay voice. Coffee cups tinkled on a little low table near Mrs. Corrie's chair. "I'm glad you're tall. Kummel?"

"She doesn't know German pronunciation," thought Miriam complacently.

"I suppose I am," she said, accepting a transparent little cup and refusing the liqueur. Those strange eyes were blue with dark rings round the iris and there were fine deep wrinkles about the mouth and chin. She looked so picturesque sitting there, like something by an "old master," but worn and tired. Why was she so happy—if she thought so many things were deadly awful....

"How's Gabbie Anstruther?"

"Oh—you see—I don't know Mrs. Anstruther. They are patients of my future brother-in-law. It was all arranged by letter."

"About your comin' here, you mean. I say—you'll never get engaged, will you? Promise?"

Miriam got up out of her deep chair and stood with her elbow on the low mantel staring into the fire. She heard phrases from Mrs. Anstruther's letter to Bennett as if they were being spoken by a tiresome grave voice. "She doats upon her children. What she really wants is someone to control her; read Shakespeare to her and get her into the air." Mrs. Corrie did not want Shakespeare. That was quite clear. And it was quite clear that she wanted a plain dull woman she could count on; always there, in a black dress. She doated. Someone else, working for her, in her pay, would look after the children and do the hard work.

"The kiddies were 'riffickly 'cited. Wanted to stay up. I hope you're strict, very strict, eh?"

"I believe I'm supposed to understand discipline," said Miriam stiffly, gazing with weary eyes at the bars of the grate.

"We were in an awful fix before we heard about you. Poor old Bunnikin breakin' down. She adored them—they're angels. But she hadn't the tiniest bit of a hold over them. Used to cry when they were naughty. *You* know. Poor old kiddies. Want them to be awfully clever. Work like a house afire. I know you're clever. P'raps you won't stay with my little heathens. Do try and stay. I can see you've got just what they want. Strong-minded, eh? I'm an imbecile. So was poor old Bunnikin. D'you like kiddies?"

"Oh, I'm very fond of children," said Miriam despairingly. She stared at the familiar bars. They were the bars of the old breakfast-room grate at home, and the schoolroom bars at Banbury Park. There they were again hard and black in the hard black grate in the midst of all this light and warmth and fragrance. Nothing had really changed. Black and hard. Someone's grate. She was alone again. Mrs. Corrie would soon find out. "I think children are so *interesting*," she said conversationally, struck by a feeling of originality in the remark. Perhaps children were interesting. Perhaps she would manage to find the children interesting. She glanced round at Mrs. Corrie. Her squarish white face was worn. Her eyes and neck looked as though all the life and youth had been washed away from them by some long sorrow. Her smile was startling ... absolute confidence and admiration ... like mother. But she would find out if one were not really interested.

5

That night Miriam roamed about her room from one to another of the faintly patterned blue hangings. Again and again she faced each one of them. For long she contemplated the drapery of the window space, the strange forest-like confusion made in the faint pattern of tiny leaves and flowers by the many soft folds, and turned from it for a distant view of the draperies of the bed and the French wardrobe. Sitting down by the fire at last she had them all in her mind's eye. She was going to be with them all night. If she stayed with them long enough she would wake one day with red bronze hair and a pale face and thin white hands. And by that time life would be all strange draperies and strange inspiring food and mocking laughing people who floated about hiding a great secret and servants who were in the plot, admiring and serving it and despising as much as anybody the vulgar things outside.

Her black dress mocked at these thoughts and she looked about for her luggage. Finding the Saratoga trunk behind the draperies of the French wardrobe she extracted her striped flannelette dressing-gown and presently sat down again with loosened hair. Entrenched in her familiar old dressing-gown, she felt more completely the power of her surroundings. Whatever should happen in this strange house she had sat for one evening in possession of this room. It was added for ever to the other things. And this one evening was more real than all the fifteen months at Banbury Park. It was so far away from everything, trams and people and noise—it was in the centre of beautiful exciting life; perfectly still and secure. Creeping to the window she held back the silk-corded rim of a curtain—a deep window-seat, a row of oblong lattices with leaded diamond panes. One of the windows was hasped a few inches open. No sound came in ... soft moist air and the smell of trees. Nothing but woods all round, everywhere.

6

The next morning a housemaid tapped at Miriam's door half an hour after she had called her to say that her breakfast was laid in the schoolroom. Going out on to the landing she discovered the room by a curious rank odour coming towards her through a half-opened door. Pushing open the door she found a large clear room, barely furnished, carpeted with linoleum and cold in the morning light pouring through an undraped window. In the grate smoked a half-ignited fire and one corner of the hearth-rug caught by a foot lay turned back. Across one end of the baize-covered table a cloth was laid, and on it stood a small crowded tray: a little teapot, no cosy, some rather thick slices of bread and butter, a small dish of marmalade, a small plate and cup and saucer piled together, and a larger plate on which lay an unfamiliar fish, dark brown, curiously dried and twisted and giving out a strong salt smoky odour. Miriam sat uncomfortably on the edge of a cane chair getting through her bread and butter and tea and one mouthful of the strong dry fish, feeling, with the door still standing wide, like a traveller snatching a hasty meal at a buffet. She tried to collect her thoughts on education. Little querulous excited sounds came to her from across the wide landing. Presently there came the swift flountering of a print dress across the landing and Wiggerson, long and willowy and capless with a cold red nose and large red hands, her thin small head looking very young with its revealed bunch of untidy hair, appeared in the schoolroom doorway with an unconscious smile hesitating on her pale lips and in her pale blue eyes. "It isn't very comfortable for you," she said in a hurried voice. "I say, my *word*"; she went to the chilly grate and bent down for the poker. Miriam glanced at the solicitous droop of her long figure. "Stokes hasn't half laid it," went on Wiggerson; "if I were you I should have breakfast in my room. They all do, except Mr. Corrie when he's at home. The other young lady was daily; she didn't stop. I should, if I were you," she finished, getting lightly to her feet. She stood between the door and the fireplace, half turned away, and gazing into space with her pale strong eyes, every line in her long pure unconscious figure waiting for Miriam's response.

"Do you *like* me, Wiggerson?" said Miriam within, "you'll have toothache and neuralgia with that thin head. You're devoted to your relations. You've got a tiresome sickly old mother. You'll never know you're a servant...." "I think perhaps I will," she drawled, clearing her throat.

"All right," said Wiggerson, with a lit face. "I'll tell them."

CHAPTER II

1

As Miriam sat having tea with the children in the dining-room the brougham drove up to the door. "There's someone arriving," she said, hoping to distract the attention of the children from her fumblings with the teapot and the hot water jug. They had certainly never met anyone who did not know how to pour out tea. But they were taken in by her bored tone.

"It's only Joey," said Sybil, frowning tranquilly, her lively penetrating brown eyes fixed on the table just ahead of the small plate nearly covered by a mass of raspberry jam from which she ate with a teaspoon in the intervals of taking small bites from a thin piece of bread and butter held conveniently near her mouth as she sat with one elbow on the table. "She's always here." She looked across the table and met the soft brown eyes of the boy. They had been wandering absently about her square pale face and her short straggling red hair as she answered Miriam. "Jenooshalet," he said, lisping over the s and smiling meditatively.

"Jeno*ash*," responded Sybil, and they both laughed drunkenly.

"What *I'm* finking," said the boy, putting a teaspoonful of jam into his teacup and speaking with a stammering difficulty that drew deep lines in his thin face; "what's worrying me is she'll have Rollo after tea instead of us.... Vat's what I'm finking."

"D'you like bays?" said Sybil, throwing a fleeting glance in the direction of Miriam.

"Yes, I do, I think," said Miriam at random, patting her hair and wondering if the children had been to Weymouth.

"Oh, *Boy*." Sybil flung her arms tightly round her thin body and sat grinning at her brother. Her old blue and white striped overall, her sparse hair and the ugly large gap between her two large front teeth seemed to set her apart from her surroundings. For a moment it seemed to Miriam that the large quiet room looking through two high windows on to a stretch of tree-shaded lawn, the cheerful little spread of delicate white china at one end of the long table, the preserves and cakes, the cress sandwiches and thin bread and butter were all there for her appreciation alone, the children somehow profane and accidental, having no right to be there. But they had been in these surroundings, the girl for twelve the boy for eight years. They had never known anything else. For years life had been for them just what it was to-day—breakfast in bed, chirping at their mother from the dressing-rooms where they slept, and scolding at Stokes as she waited on their toilet; jocularly and impatiently learning lessons from little text-books for an hour or so in the morning, spending their afternoons cantering about the commons and along the sandy roadways with the groom; driving with their mother or walking with the governess and every day coming in at the end of the afternoon to this cosy, dainty grown-up tea, with their strange untroubled brooding faces. They would grow up and be exactly like their parents. They did not know anything about their fate. It was a kind of prison. Perhaps they knew. Perhaps that was what they were always brooding over. No, they did not mind. Their musings were tranquil. They were waiting. They had silent conversations all the time. To be with them after being so long with the straining, determined, secretly ambitious children at Banbury Park was a great relief ... the way they moved their heads and used their hands ... the boy's hands were wonderful, the palest fine brown silk, quick eloquent little claws, promising understanding and support. Fine little hands and steady gentle brown eyes.

"Bays."

"*Bright* bays."

"Roans."

"*Strawberry* roans."

"*Chestnuts.*"

"*Chestnut* bays."

The children sat facing each other, each with clasped hands, and eyes lit with dreams. Miriam listened. Bay, then, must be that curious liver colour that was neither brown nor chestnut.

"Our ponies are bay," said Sybil quickly, with flushed face. "Boy's and mine, the brougham and victoria horses are chestnut bays and we've got two dogs, a whippet bitch, she's in the stables now, and a Great Dane; I'm going to have a Willoughby pug pup on my birthday."

2

Mrs. Corrie was standing in the hall when the little tea-party came out of the dining-room. She raised her head and stood shaped in the well-cut lines of her long brown and fawn check coat and skirt against the bead curtain that led to the drawing-room, looking across at them. The boy tottered blindly across the hall with arms outstretched. "Oh, Rollo, Rollo," he said brokenly, as he reached her, pressing his hands up against her grey suède waistcoat and his face into her skirt, "are we going to h—*ave* you?"

Mrs. Corrie began singing in a thin laughing voice, taking the boy by the wrists.

"No, no," he said sharply, "let me hold you a minute." But Mrs. Corrie danced, forcing his steps as he pressed against her. Up and down the hall they capered while Sybil pranced round them whirling her skirts and clapping her hands. Miriam sank into a settee. The cold March sunlight streaming in through the thinly curtained windows painted the sharply bobbing figures in faint shadows on the wall opposite her.

3

When the dancers were breathless the little party strayed into the drawing-room. Presently they were gathered at the piano. Mrs. Corrie sat on a striped ottoman and peering closely picked out the airs of songs that made Miriam stare in amazement. They all sang. Slowly and stumblingly with many gasps of annoyance from Mrs. Corrie and the children violently assaulting each other whenever either of them got ahead of the halting accompaniment, they sang through all the songs in an album with a brightly decorated paper cover. But in their performance there was no tune, no rhythm, and the words spoken out slowly and separately were intolerable to her. One song they sang three times. Its chorus

Stiboo—stib*ee*,

Sti-ibbety-*oo*

Sti-ibbety-b*oo*,

Stib*ee*,

which Sybil could sing without the piano with an extraordinary flourishing rapidity, pirouetting as she sang, they attacked again and again, slowly and waveringly, fitting the syllables note by note into the printed line of disconnected jerkily tailed quavers.... They thought this was music. Encouraged at last by the fervour of the halting performance Miriam found herself seated at the piano attacking the score. They went through the songs from the beginning, three thin blissful wavering tremulous voices, with a careful perfect monotony of emphasis, uninfluenced by any variation of accent or inflection introduced by Miriam into the accompaniment. Looking round as they reached the end she saw flushed rapt faces with happy eyes gleaming through the gathering twilight. They smiled at her as they sang. When they had finished they lit the piano candles and sang "Stiboo" once more.

4

"Sti-boo, stibee, sti-ibbety-oo, sti-ibbety boo, stibee," sang Miriam, getting into the large square bodice of her silkette evening dress. Its great oblong box-like elbow sleeves more than filled the mirror as she stood. They were stiffened with stout muslin, and stood squarely out from shoulder to elbow, so that the little band of silk edged with a piping of salmon pink velveteen which held them round the arm just above the elbow could only be seen when she raised her arms. The piping was repeated round the square neck of her bodice, cutting in front across the bust just below the collar bone and at the back just above her shoulder blades. She sang the little refrain at intervals until her toilet was completed by the pinning of a small salmon pink velvet bow against the left side of the hard mass of her coiled hair and went humming downstairs into the hall. The soles of her new patent leather shoes felt pleasantly smooth against the thick carpet. She went across the hall to prop a foot against the fender and take one more reassuring look at the little disc of steel beads adorning her toe. "Stiboo——"

"Won't you come in here?" said a soft staccato bass voice, a woman's voice, but deep and rounded like the voice of a deep-chested watch-dog barking single soft notes after a furious outbreak.

Miriam looked round. Wiggerson was lighting the big lamp in the dining-room, peering up under the rose-coloured shade. "In here," repeated the deep voice, smiling, and Miriam's eyes discovered that the small door set back between the dining-room and the window on the left side of the hall door was open, showing part of a curious soft brown room; a solid brown leather covered secretaire, with a revolving chair between its pillars of drawers, set back in the bow of a small window, a little bronze lamp with a plain buff-coloured shade standing near a pile of large volumes on the secretaire, a piece of wall covered with a dark silky-looking brown paper shining in the glow of an invisible fire. She went forward across the hall into the room with a polite pleased hesitating smile. There was a faint rich exciting odour in the warm little room ... cigars ... leather ... a sort of deep freedom. The rest of the house seemed suddenly far away. Coloured drawings of houses on the little brown walls, two enormous deep low leather arm-chairs drawn up on either side of an enormous fire, a littered mantelshelf. "I saw you froo the crack," said a lady, fitted deeply into one of the large chairs. She held out a small hand when Miriam was near enough to take it and said softly and lazily, "You're the new guvnis, aren't you? I'm Joey Banks."

"Yes, I came yesterday," said Miriam serenely.

Sinking into the second arm-chair she crossed her knees and beamed into the fire. What perfect security.... She turned to Mr. Corrie, unknown and mysteriously away somewhere in London to thank him for setting her here, protected from the whole world in the deeps of his study chair—all the worry and the noise and the fussing people shut away. If suddenly he came in she would not thank him, but he would know. He would be sitting in the other arm-chair, and she would say, "What do you think about everything?" Not so much to hear what he thought, but because some of his thoughts would be her thoughts. Thought was the same in everybody who thought at all. She would sit back and rest and hear an understanding voice. He might be heavy and fat. But a leading Q.C. must have thoughts ... and he had been thin once ... and there were those books ... and he would read newspapers; perhaps too many newspapers. He would know almost at once that she thought he read too many newspapers. She would have to conceal that to hear the voice going on and leaving her undisturbed.

5

Of course people like this wore evening dress every day. You could only rest and think and talk and be happy without collars and sleeves—with the cool beaded leather against one's neck and arms in the firelight....

She gazed familiarly into her companion's eyes taking in her soft crimson silk evening dress with its wide folded belt of black velvet and the little knots of black about the square sleeves, as the eyes smiled long and easily into hers ... the smile of one of the girls at the Putney school, the same dark fringed caressing smiling eyes set in delicately bulging pale brown cheeks, the same little frizz of dark hair. She felt for the name, but could only recall the sense of the girl as she had sat, glints of fear and hard watchfulness in the beautiful eyes, trying to copy her neighbour's exercise. This girl's dull hair was fluffed cloudily, and there was no uneasiness in the eyes. Probably she too had been a duffer at school and had had to crib things. But she had left all that behind and her smile was—perfect.

"You look like an Oriental princess," said Miriam, gazing.

Joey flushed and smiled more deeply, but without making the smallest movement.

"Do I, weally?"

"Exactly," said Miriam, keeping her own pose with difficulty. She knew she had flung up her head and spoken emphatically. But the girl was such a wonderful effect—she wanted her to be able to see herself ... she was not quite of the same class as the Corries, or different, somehow. Miriam gazed on. Raising the large black cushion a little, turning her head and pressing her cheek into it, her eyes still on Miriam's, Joey laughed a short contralto gurgle, bringing the sharp dimples and making her cheeks bulge slightly on either side of the chin.

"I brought it in from Rollo's room," she said. "I like bein' in here. Rollo never comes in; but she always has a fire in here when she's got people stoppin'. You can pop in here whenever you like when Felix isn't at home. It's jolly. I like it."

Miriam looked into the fire and thought. Joey, too, liked talking to Mr. Corrie in his room when he was not there. He must be one of those charming sort of men, rather weak, who went on liking people. Joey was evidently an old friend of the family and still liked him. She evidently liked even to mention his name. He couldn't be really anything much ... or perhaps Joey didn't really know him at all. Joey did not live there. She came and went.

"Of course you haven't seen Felix yet, have you?"

"No."

Joey straightened her head on her pillow.

"It's not the least use me tryin' to describe him to you," she breathed in broken tones.

Miriam struggled uneasily with her thoughts ... a leading Q.C.—about forty.... "Oh, do try," she said, a little fearfully ... how vulgar ... just like a housemaid ... no; Wiggerson would never have said such a thing, nor asked at all. It was treachery to Mr. Corrie. If Joey said anything more about him she would never be able to speak to him freely.

"He's divine," said Joey, smiling into the fire.

How nice of Joey to be so free with her and want her to like him too ... the gong. They both rose and peered into the little strip of mirror in the small overmantel ... divine might mean anything ... divine ... oh, quite too utterly too-too ... greenery-yellery—Grosvenor-gallery—foot-in-the-grave young man.

CHAPTER III

1

The next day the ground was powdered with snow. Large snowflakes were hurrying through the air driving to and fro on a harsh wind. The wind snored round the house like a flame and bellowed in the chimneys. An opened window let in the cold air and the smell of the snow. No sound came from the woods. The singing of the birds and the faint sound of the woods had gone.

But when Miriam left her room to go across to the schoolroom and wait for the children she found the spring in the house. The landing was bright with the light streaming through many open doors. Rooms were being prepared. On a large tray on the landing table lay a mass of spring flowers and little flowered bowls of many shapes and sizes filled with fresh water. Stokes and Wiggerson were fluttering in and out of the rooms carrying frilled bed-linen, lace-edged towels and flowered bed-spreads.

People with money could make the spring come as soon as the days lengthened. Clear bright rooms, bright clean paint, soft coloured hangings, spring flowers in the bright light on landings. The warmth from stoves and fires seemed as if it came from the sun. Its glow changed suddenly to the glow of sunlight. It drew the scent of the flowers into the air. And with the new scent of the new flowers something was moving and leaping and dancing in the air. Outside the wintry weather might go on and on as though the spring would never come.

In a dull cheap villa there might be a bunch of violets in a bowl on a whatnot. Snuffing very close you could feel the tide of spring wash through your brain. But only in the corner where the violets were. In cold rooms upstairs you could remember the violets and the spring; but the spring did not get into the house.

There was an extraordinary noise going on downstairs. Standing inside the schoolroom door Miriam listened. Joey's contralto laugh coming up in gusts, the sound of dancing feet, the children shouting names, Mrs. Corrie repeating them in her laughing wavering chalky voice. Joey; certainly Joey was not dancing about. She was probably sitting on the sofa watching them, and thinking. Fancy their being so excited about people coming. Just like any ordinary people. She went into the schoolroom saying over the names to herself. "Mélie to-day ... Dad and Mr. Staple-Craven to-morrow ... the Bean-pole for Sunday" ... someone they knew very well. It might be either a tall man or a tall woman.... They made the house spring-like because people were coming. Would the people notice that the house was spring-like? Would they *realise*? People did not seem to realise anything. They would patronise the flowers ... they ought to feel wild with joy; join hands and dance round the flowers.

At lunch time the door at the far end of the dining-room stood open showing the shrouded length of a billiard-table, and beyond it at the far end in the gloom a squat oak chimney-piece littered with pipes and other small objects. The light, even from the overcast sky, came in so brilliantly that the holland cover looked almost white. There must be several windows; perhaps three. What a room to have, just for a billiard-room. A quiet, mannish room, waiting until it was wanted, the pockets of the table bulging excitingly under the cover, the green glass supports under the squat round stoutly spindling legs, a bit of a huge armchair showing near the fireplace, the end of a sofa, the green shaded lamps low over the table, the dark untidy mantelpiece, tobacco, books, talks, billiards. In there too the spring flowers stood ready on the table. They would be put somewhere on the wide dark mantel, probably on a corner out of the way. "We used to play table billiards at home," said Miriam at random, longing to know what part the billiard-room played in the week-end.

"Billy-billy," said Mrs. Corrie, "oh, we'll have some fun. We'll *all* play."

"It was *such* a bore stretching the webbing," said Miriam critically, avoiding Sybil's eager eyes.

"It *must* have been—but how awfully jolly to have billiards. I simply adaw billiards," said Joey fervently.

"Such a fearful business getting them absolutely taut," pursued Miriam, feeling how much the cream caramel was enhanced by the sight of the length, beyond the length of the dining-room, of that bright long heavy room. She imagined it lit and people walking about amongst the curious lights and shadows with cues—and cigarettes; quiet intent faces. Englishmen. Did the English invent billiards?

"Poor old Joey. Wish you weren't going to the dentist. You won't be here when Mélie comes."

"Don't mind the dentist a scrap. I'm looking forward to it. I shall see Mélie to-night."

, She doesn't like her, thought Miriam; people being together is awful; like the creaking of furniture.

2

Mélie arrived an hour before dinner time. Miriam heard Mrs. Corrie taking her into the room next to her own with laughter and many phrases. A panting, determined voice, like a voice out of a play, the thick, smooth, rather common voice of a fair-haired middle-aged lady in a play kept saying, "The pores, my dear. I must open my pores after the journey. I'm *choked* with it."

Presently Mélie's door closed and Mrs. Corrie tapped and put her head inside Miriam's door. "She's goin' to have a steam bath on her floor, got an injarubber tent on the floor and a spirit lamp. She's gettin' inside it. Isn't she an old *cure!*"

"She's thinking more about her food than anything they're saying; she doesn't really care about them a bit," thought Miriam at dinner, gazing again and again across at Mrs. Staple-Craven's fat little shape seated opposite herself in a tightly fitting pale blue silk dress whose sleeves had tiny puffs instead of the fashionable large square sleeves. Watching her cross unconscious face, round and blue-eyed and all pure "milk and roses," her large yellow head with a tiny twist of hair standing up like the handle of a jug, exactly on the top of the crown, her fat white hands with thick soft curly fingers and bright pink nails, the strange blue stare that went from thing to thing on the table, hearing her thick smooth heedless voice, with its irrelevant assertions and statements, Miriam wondered how she had come to be Mrs. Staple-Craven. She was no more Mrs. Staple-Craven than she was sitting at Mrs. Corrie's table. She was not really there. She was just getting through, and neither Mrs. Corrie nor Joey really knew this. At the same time she was too stout and gluttonous to be still really a fairy in Devonshire. Where was she? What did she think? She went on and on because she was afraid someone might ask her that.

Although Joey had been to have her hair dyed and had not been to the dentist at all she was not pretending nearly so much. She was a little ashamed. Why had she said she was going to the dentist and come back with sheeny bronzy hair, ashamed? She had been worrying about her looks. Perhaps she was more than twenty-one. Nan Babington said no one need mind being twenty-one if they were engaged, but if not it was a frantic age to be. Joey was a poor worried thing, just like any other girl.

3

When they were safely ensconced round the drawing-room fire Mrs. Staple-Craven sat very upright in her chair with her plump little hands on either arm and her eyes fixed on the blaze. Joey pleading toothache had said good night and gone away with her coffee. There was a moment's silence.

"You'd never think I'd been fairly banged to death by the spirits last night," said Mrs. Staple-Craven in a thick flat reproachful narrative tone. It sounds like a housekeeper giving an order to a servant she knows won't obey her, thought Miriam, swishing more comfortably into her chair. If Mrs. Craven would talk there would be no need to do anything.

"Ah-ha," said Mrs. Craven, still looking at the fire, "something's pleasing Miss Henderson."

"Is she rejoicin'? Tell us about the spirits, Mélie. I'm deadly keen. Deadly. She mustn't be too delighted. I've told her she's not to get engaged."

"Engaged?" enquired Mrs. Craven, of the fire.

"She's promised," said Mrs. Corrie, turning off the lights until only one heavily shaded lamp was left, throwing a rosy glow over Mélie's compact form.

"She won't, if she's not under the star, to be sure."

"Oh, she mustn't think about stars. Why should she marry?"

Miriam looked a little anxiously from one to the other.

"You've shocked her, Julia," said Mrs. Staple-Craven. "Never mind at all, my dear. You'll marry if you're under the star."

"Star, star, beautiful star, a handsome one with twenty thousand a year," sang Mrs. Corrie.

"I don't think a man has any right to be handsome," said Miriam desperately—she must manage to keep the topic going. These women were so terrible—they filled her with fear. She must make them take back what they had said.

"A handsome man's much handsomer than a pretty woman," said Mrs. Craven.

"It's cash, cash, cash—that's what it is," chanted Mrs. Corrie softly.

"Oh, do you?" said Miriam. "I think a handsome man's generally so weak."

Mrs. Craven stared into the fire.

"You take the one who's got the ooftish, my friend," said Mrs. Corrie.

"But you say I'm not to marry."

"You shall marry when my poor little old kiddies are grown up. We'll find you a very nice one with plenty of money."

"Then you *don't* think marriage is a failure," said Miriam, with immense relief.

Mrs. Corrie leaned towards her with laughter in her clear light eyes. It seemed to fill the room. "Have some more coffy-drink?"

"No, thanks," said Miriam, shivering.

"Sing us something—she sings, Mélie—German songs. Isn't she no end clever?"

"Does she?" said Mrs. Craven. "Yes. She's got a singing chin. Sing us a pretty song, my dear."

As she fluttered the leaves of her Schumann album she saw Mrs. Craven sit back with closed eyes, and Mrs. Corrie still sitting forward in her chair with her hands clasped on her knees gazing with a sad white face into the flames.

"Ich grolle nicht, und wenn das Herz auch bricht," sang Miriam, and thought of Germany. Her listeners did not trouble her. They would not understand. No English person would quite understand—the need, that the Germans understood so well—the need to admit the beauty of things ... the need of the strange expression of music, making the beautiful things more beautiful and of words when they were together in the beauty of the poems. Music and poetry told everything—whether you understood the music or the words—they put you in the mood that made things shine—then heart-break or darkness did not matter. Things go on shining in the end; German landscapes and German sunshine and German towns were full of this knowledge. In England there was something besides—something hard.

"'Menjous, ain't it?" said Mrs. Corrie, as she rose from the piano.

"If we lived aright we should all be singing," said Mrs. Craven, "it's natural."

4

"You look a duck."

Miriam stood still at the top of the stairs and looked down into the hall. Mrs. Staple-Craven was standing under the largest lamp near the fireplace looking up at a tall man in a long ulster. Grizzled hair and a long face with a long pointed grizzled beard—she was staring up at him with her eyes "like saucers" and her face pink, white, gold, "like a full moon"—how awful for him ... he'd come down from town probably in a smoking carriage, talking, and there she was and he had to say something.

"I've just had my bath," said Mrs. Craven, without altering the angle of her gaze.

"You look a duck," said the tall man fussily, half turning away.

Standing with his back to the couple, opening letters at the hall table was a little man in a neat little overcoat with a silk hat tilted back on his head. His figure had a curious crooked jaunty appearance, the shoulders a little crooked and the little legs slightly bent. "It's Mr. Corrie," mused Miriam, moving backwards as he turned and went swiftly out banging the front door behind him. "He looks like a jockey"; she got herself back into her room until the hall should be clear. "He's gone down to the stables." She listened to the quick jerky little footsteps crunching along the gravel outside her window.

Soon after the quick little steps sounded on the stairs and the children shouted from their rooms. A door was opened and shut and for five minutes there was a babel of voices. Then the steps came out again and went away down the passage leading off the landing to the bathroom and a little spare room at the further end. They passed the bathroom and the door of the little room was opened and shut and locked. Everything was silent in the house, but from the room next to hers came the sounds of Mr. Craven plunging quickly about and blowing and clearing his throat. She had not heard him come up.

When at last she came downstairs she found the whole party standing talking in the hall. The second gong was drowning the terrible voices, leaving nothing but gesticulating figures. Presently Mr. Staple-Craven was standing before her with Mrs. Corrie, and her hand was powerfully wrung and released with a fussy emphatic handshake cancelling the first impression. Mr. Craven made some remark in a high voice, lost by Miriam as Mr. Corrie came across to her from talking to Joey under a lamp and took her hand. "Let me introduce your host," he said, keeping her hand and placing it on his arm as he turned towards the dining-room, "and take you in to dinner."

Miriam went across the hall past the servants waiting on either side of the dining-room door and down the long room with her hand on the soft coat sleeve of a neat little dinner jacket and her footsteps led by the firm, disconnected, jumpy footsteps of the little figure at her side. There was a vague crowd of people coming along behind. "Come on, everybody," Mrs. Corrie had pealed delicately, and Mrs. Craven had said in a thick smooth explanatory voice, "Of course she's the greatest stranger."

The table was set with replicas of the little groups of Venetian wine and finger glasses and fine silver and cutlery that had accompanied Miriam's first sense of dining and when she found herself seated at Mr. Corrie's left hand opposite Mrs. Craven, with Joey away on her left, facing Mr. Craven and Mrs. Corrie now far away from her at the door end of the table, it seemed as if these things had been got together only for the use of the men. Why were women there? Why did men and women dine together? She would have liked to sit there and watch and listen, but not to dine—not to be seen dining by Mr. Corrie. It was extraordinary, this muddle of men and women with nothing in common. The men must hate it. She knew he did not have such thoughts. All the decanters stood in a little group between him and the great bowl of flaring purple and crimson anemones that stood in the centre of the table, and the way in which he said when her soup came, "Have some Moselle," and filled her glass, compelled her to feel welcome to share the ritual of the feast. She sat with bent head wrapped and protected, hearing nothing as the voices sounded about the table but the clear sweet narrow rather drawling tones of Mr. Corrie's voice. She could hear it talking to men, on racecourses, talking in clubs, laughing richly, rather drunkenly, at improper stories in club smoking-rooms; dining, talking and lunching, dining, talking, talking every day and sitting there now, wonderfully, giving her security. She knew with perfect certainty that nothing painful or disagreeable or embarrassing could come near her in his presence. But he knew nothing about her; much less than Wiggerson knew.

5

Joey felt the same, of course. But Joey was laughing and talking in her deep voice and making eyes. No, it was not the same. Joey was not happy.

These people sitting at his table were supposed to be friends. But they knew nothing about him. He made little quiet mocking jokes and laughed and kept things going. The Staple-Cravens knew nothing at all about him. Mrs. Staple-Craven did not care for anybody. She looked about and always spoke as if she were answering an accusation that nobody had made—a dressmaker persuading you to have something and talking on and on in fat tones to prevent your asking the price.... Mr. Craven only cared for himself. He was weak and pompous and fussy with a silly elaborate chivalrous manner. There was a stillness round the table. Miriam felt that it centred in her and was somehow her fault. Never mind. She had successfully got through whitebait and a quail. She would write home about the quails and whitebait and the guests and say nothing about her own silence—"Mr. Staple-Craven is a poet ..."

"Give Mélie some more drink, Percy," said Mrs. Corrie. "It's all wrong you two sittin' together."

"She likes to sit near me, don't you, my duck?" said Mr. Craven, looking about for the wine and bowing to and fro from his hips.

"You've been away so long," murmured Mr. Corrie. "What sort of a place is Balone to stay in?"

"Oh, nothing of a place in itself, nothing of a place. Why do you call it Balone?"

"Isn't that right? That's right enough. Come."

Miriam waited eagerly, her eyes on Mr. Craven's pink face with the grizzled hair above and below it. How perfectly awful he must look in his nightshirt, she thought, and flushed violently. "Balloyne," he was saying carefully, showing his red lips and two rows of unnaturally even teeth.... "Oh, Lord, they mean Bologne." Both men were talking together. "Balloyne is perfectly correct; the correct pronunciation," said Mr. Craven in a loud testy voice, with loose lips. Mrs. Craven gazed up ... like a distressed fish ... into his flushed face. Mrs. Corrie was throwing out her little wavering broken laughs. Keeping his angry voice Mr. Craven went on. Miriam sat eagerly up and glanced at Mr. Corrie. He was sitting with his lips drawn down and his eyebrows raised ... his law-court face.... Suddenly his face relaxed and the dark boyish brown head with the clear thoughtful brow and the gentle kind eyes turned towards her. "Let's ask Miss Henderson. She shall be umpire."

6

Miriam carefully enunciated the word. The blood sang in her ears as everyone looked her way. The furniture and all the room mimicked her. What did it matter, after all, the right pronunciation? It did matter; not that Balone was wrong, but the awfulness of being able to miss the right sound if you had once heard it spoken. There was some awful meaning in the way English people missed the right sound; all the names in India, all the Eastern words. How *could* an English traveller hear hahreem, and speak it hairum, Aswân and say Ass-ou-ann? It made them miss other things and think wrongly about them. "That's more like it," she heard Mr. Corrie say. There was sheeny braiding round the edges of his curious little coat. "Got you there, Craven, got you there," he was saying somewhere in his mind ... his mind went on by itself repeating things wearily. His small austere face shone a little with dining; the corners of his thin lips slackened. "I can read all your thoughts. None of you can disturb my enjoyment of this excellent dinner; none of you can enhance it" ... but he was not quite conscious of his thoughts. Why did not the others read them? Perhaps they did. Perhaps they were too much occupied to notice what people were thinking. Perhaps in society people always were. The Staple-Cravens did not notice. But they were neither of them quite sure of themselves. Mrs. Corrie was busy all the time dancing and singing somewhere alone, wistfully. Joey kept throwing her smile at Mr. Corrie—lounging a little, easily, over the table and saying in her mind, "I understand you, the others don't, I do," and he smiled at her, broadened the smile that had settled faintly all over his face, now and again in her direction. But she did not understand him. "Divine," perhaps he was, or could be. But Joey did not know him. She only knew that he had a life of his own and no one else at the table had quite completely. She did not know that with all his worldly happiness and success and self-control he was miserable and lost and needing consolation ... but neither did he. Perhaps he never would; would not find it out because he had so many thoughts and was always talking. So he thought he liked Joey. Because she smiled and responded. "Jabez Balfour," he was saying slowly, savouring the words and smiling through his raised wineglass with half closed eyes. That was for Mr. Staple-Craven; there was some exciting secret in it. Presently they would be two men over their wine and nuts. Mr. Staple-Craven took this remark for himself at once, scorning the women with a thick polite insolence. His lips shot out. "Ah," he said busily, "Jabez Balfour, Jabez Balfour; ah," he swung from side to side from his waist. "Let me see, Jabez...."

"The Liberator scheme," said Mr. Corrie interestedly with a bright young eye. "They've got 'im this time; fairly got 'im on the hop."

Jabez Balfour; what a beautiful name. He could not have done anything wrong. There was a soft glare of anger in Mr. Corrie's eyes; as if he were accusing Mr. Staple-Craven of some crime, or everybody. Perhaps one would hear something about crime; crime. That's crime—somebody taking down a book and saying triumphantly, "that's crime," and people talking excitedly about it, in the warm, at dinners ... like that moment at Richmond Park, the ragged man with panting mouth, running ... the quiet grass, the scattered deer, the kindly trees, the gentlemen with triumphant faces, running after him; enough, enough, he had suffered enough ... his poor face, their dreadful faces. He knew more than they did. Crime could not be allowed. People murdering you in your sleep. But criminals knew that—the running man knew. He was running away from himself. He knew he had spoiled the grass and the trees and the deer. To have stopped him and hidden him and let him get over it. His poor face.... The awful moment of standing up trying to say or do something, feeling so weak, trembling at the knees, the man's figure pelting along in the distance, the two gentlemen passing, their white waistcoats, homes, wives, bathrooms, stuffiness, indigestion....

7

"It comes perfectly into line with Biblical records, my dear Corrie: a single couple, two cells originating the whole creation."

"I'm maintaining that's not the Darwinian idea at all. It was not a single couple, but several different ones."

"We're not descended from monkeys at all. It's not natural," said Mrs. Craven loudly, across the irritated voices of the men. Their faces were red. They filled the room with inaccurate phrases pausing politely between each and keeping up a show of being guest and host. How nice of them. But this was how cultured people with incomes talked about Darwin.

"The great thing Darwin did," said Miriam abruptly, "was to point out the power of environment in evolving the different species—selecting."

"That's it, that's it!" sang Mrs. Corrie. "Let's all select ourselves into the droin'-room." "Now I've offended the men and the women too," thought Miriam.

8

Mr. Staple-Craven joined the ladies almost at once. He came in leaving the door open behind him and took a chair in the centre of the fireside circle and sat giving little gasps and sighs of satisfaction, spreading his hands and making little remarks about the colours of the fire, and the shape of the coffee cups. There he was and he would have to be entertained, although he had nothing at all to say and was puzzling about himself and life all the time behind his involuntary movements and polite smiles and gestures. Perhaps he was uneasy because he knew there was someone saying all the time, "You're a silly pompous old man and you think yourself much cleverer than you are." But it was not altogether that; he was always uneasy, even when he was alone, unless he was rapidly preparing to go and be with people who did not know what he was. If he had been alone with the other three women he would have forgotten for a while and half-liked, half-despised them for their affability.

"The great man's always at work, always at work," he said suddenly, in a desperate sort of way. They were like some sort of needlework guild sitting round, just people, in the end; it made the surroundings seem quite ordinary. The room fell to pieces; one could imagine it being turned out, or all the things being sold up and dispersed.

"All work and no play," scolded Mrs. Craven, "makes Jack...."

Miriam heard the swish of the bead curtain at the end of the short passage.

"Heah he *is*," smiled Joey.

"A miracle," breathed Mrs. Craven, glancing round the circle. Evidently he did not usually come in.

Mr. Corrie came quietly into the room with empty hands; in the clear light he looked older than he had done in the dining-room, fuller in the face; grey threads showed in his hair. Everyone turned towards him. He looked at no one. His loose little smile had gone. The straight chair into which he dropped with a dreamy careless preoccupied air was set a little back from the fireside circle. No one moved.

"Absorbed the evidence, m'lud?" squeaked Mr. Craven.

"Ah-m," growled his host, clearing his throat.

Why can't they let him alone, Miriam asked herself, and leave him to me, added her mind swiftly. She sat glaring into the fire; the room had resumed its strange magic.

9

"Do you think it is wrong to teach children things you don't believe yourself?..." said Miriam, and her thoughts rushed on. "You're an unbeliever and I'm an unbeliever and both of us despise the thoughts and opinions of 'people'; you're a successful wealthy man and can amuse yourself and forget; I must teach and presently die, teach till I die. It doesn't matter. I can be happy for a while teaching your children, but you know, knowing me a little what a task that must be; you know I know nothing and that I know that nobody knows anything; comfort me...."

She seemed to traverse a great loop of time waiting for the answer to her hurried question. Mr. Corrie had come into the drawing-room dressed for dinner and sat down near her with a half-smile as she closed the book she was reading and laid it on her knee and looked up with sentences from "A Human Document" ringing through her, and by the time her question was out she knew it was unnecessary. But she had flung it out and it had reached him and he had read the rush of thoughts that followed it. She might as well have been silent; better. She had missed some sort of opportunity. What would have happened if she had been quite silent? His answer was swift, but in the interval they had said all they would ever have to say to each other. "Not in the least," he said, with a gentle decisiveness.

She flashed thanks at him and sighed her relief. He did not mind about religion. But how far did he understand? She had made him think she was earnest about the teaching children something. He would be very serious about their being "decently turned out." She was utterly incapable of turning them out for the lives they would have to lead. She envied and pitied and despised those lives. Envied the ease and despised the ignorance, the awful cruel struggle of society that they were growing up for—no joy, a career and sport for the boy, clubs, the weary dyspeptic life of the blasé man, and for the girl lonely cold hard bitter everlasting "social" life. She envied the ease. Mr. Corrie must know she envied the ease. Did he know that she tried to hide her incapacity in order to go on sharing the beauty and ease?

"It is so difficult," she pursued helplessly, and saw him wonder why she went on with the subject and try to read the title of her book. She did not mean to tell him that. That would lead them away; just nowhere. If only she could tell him everything and get him to understand. But that would mean admitting that she was letting the children's education slide; and he was sitting there, confidently, so beautifully dressed for dinner, paying her forty pounds a year not to let the children's education slide.... "It's an opportunity; he's come in here, and sat down to talk to me. I ought to tell him; I'm cheating." But he had looked for the title of her book, and would have talked, about anything, if she could have talked. He had a little air of deference, quiet kind indulgent deference. His neat little shoulders, bent as he sat turned towards her, were kind. "I'm too young," she cried in her mind. If only she could say aloud, "I'm too young—I can't do it," and leave everything to him.

Or leave the children out altogether and talk to him, man to man, about the book. She could not do that. Everything she said would hurt her, poisoned by the hidden sore of her incapability to do anything for his children. He ought to send them to school. But they would not go to a school where anything real was taught. Science, strange things about India and Ireland, the æsthetic movement, Ruskin; making things beautiful. How far away all that seemed, that sacred life of her old school—forgotten. The thought of it was like a breath in the room. Did he know of these things? That sort of school would take the children away, out of this kind of society life. Make them think—for themselves. He did not think or approve of thought. Even the hard Banbury Park people would be nearer to him than any of those things.... That was the world. Nearly everyone seemed to be in it. He was whimsically trying to read the title of her book with the little half-smile he shared with the boy.

People came in and they both rose. It was over. She sank back miserably into the offering of the moment, retiring into a lamp-lit corner with her book, enclosing herself in its promise.

10

She sat long that night over her fire dipping into the strange book, reading passages here and there; feeling them come nearer to her than anything she had read before. She knew at once that she did not want to read the book through; that it was what people called a tragedy, that the author had deliberately made it a tragedy; something black and twisted and painful, painful came to her out of every page; but seriously to read it right through and be excited about the tragic story seemed silly and pitiful. The thought of Mrs. Corrie and Joey doing this annoyed her and impatiently she wanted to tell them that there was nothing in it, nothing in the things the author wanted to make them believe; that was fraud, humbug ... they missed everything. They could not see through it, they read through to the happy ending or the sad ending and took it all seriously.

She struggled in thought to discover why it was she felt that these people did not read books and that she herself did. She felt that she could look at the end, and read here and there a little and know; know something, something they did not know. People thought it was silly, almost wrong to look at the end of a book. But if it spoilt a book, there was something wrong about the book. If it was finished and the interest gone when you know who married who, what was the good of reading at all? It was a sort of trick, a sell. Like a puzzle that was no more fun when you had found it out. There was something more in books than that ... even Rosa Nouchette Carey and Mrs. Hungerford, something that came to you out of the book, any bit of it, a page, even a sentence—and the "stronger" the author was the more came. That was why Ouida put those others in the shade, not, not, *not* because her books were improper. It was her, herself somehow. Then you read books to find the author! That was it. That was the difference ... that was how one was different from most people.... Dear Eve; I have just discovered that I don't read books for the story, but as a psychological study of the author ... she must write that to Eve at once; to-morrow. It was rather awful and strange. It meant never being able to agree with people about books, never liking them for the same reasons as other people.... But it was true and exciting. It meant ... things coming to you out of books, people, not the people in the books, but knowing, absolutely, everything about the author. She clung to the volume in her hand with a sense of wealth. Its very binding, the feeling of it, the sight of the slender serried edges of the closed leaves came to her as having a sacredness ... and the world was full of books.... It did not matter that people went about talking about nice books, interesting books, sad books, "stories"—they would never be that to her. They were people. More real than actual people. They came nearer. In life everything was so scrappy and mixed up. In a book the author was there in every word.

Why did this strange book come so near, nearer than any others, so that you *felt* the writing, felt the sentences as if you were writing them yourself? He was a sad pained man, all wrong; bothered and tragic about things, believing in sad black horror. Then why did he come so near? Perhaps because life was sad. Perhaps life was really sad. No; it was somehow the writing, the clearness. That was the thing. He himself must be all right, if he was so clear. Then it was dangerous, dangerous to people like Mrs. Corrie and Joey who would attend only to what he said, and not to him ... sadness or gladness, saying things were sad or glad did not matter; there was something behind all the time, something inside people. That was why it was impossible to pretend to sympathise with people. You don't have to sympathise with authors; you just get at them, neither happy nor sad; like talking, more than talking. Then that was why the people who wrote moral stories were so awful. They were standing behind the pages preaching at you with smarmy voices.... Bunyan?... No.... He preached to himself too ... crying out his sins.... He did not get between you and himself and point at a moral. An author must show himself. Anyhow, he can't help showing himself. A moral writer only sees the mote in his brother's eye. And you see him seeing it.

11

A long letter to Eve.... Eve would think that she was showing off. But she would be excited and interested too, and would think about it a little. If only she could make Eve see what a book was ... a dance by the author, a song, a prayer, an important sermon, a message. Books were not stories printed on paper, they were people; the real people; ... "I prefer books to people" ... "I know now why I prefer books to people."

12

"... I do wish you'd tell me more about your extraordinary days. You must have extraordinary days. I do. Perhaps everyone has. Only they don't seem to know it!"

... This morning, the green common lying under the sun, still and wide and silent; with a little breeze puffing over it; the intense fresh green near the open door of the little Catholic church; the sandy pathway running up into the common, hummocky and twisting and winding, its sand particles glinting in the sun, always there, going on, whoever died or whatever happened, winding amongst happy greenery, in and out amongst the fresh smell of the common. Inside the chapel the incense streaming softly up, the seven little red lamps hanging in the cloud of incense about the altar; the moving of the thick forest of embroidery on the cope of the priest. Funny when he bobbed, but when he just moved quietly, taking a necessary step, all the colour of the forest on his cope moving against the still high wide colours of the chancel. If only anyone could express how perfect life was at those moments; everyone must know, everyone who was looking must know that life was perfectly happy. That is why people went to church; for those moments with the light on all those things in the chancel. It meant something.... Priests and nuns knew it all the time; even when they were unhappy; that was why they could kiss dying people and lepers; they saw something else, all the time. Nothing common or unclean. That was why Christ had blazing eyes. Christianity: the sanctification of bread and wine, and lepers and death; the body; the resurrection of the body. Even if there was some confusion and squabbling about Christ there must be something in it if the things that showed were so beautiful.

Hard cold vows, of chastity and poverty. That did it. Emptiness, in face of—an unspeakable glory. If one could not, was too weak or proud, "Verily they have their reward." Everyone got something somehow ... in hell; thou art there also ... that shows there is no eternal punishment. Earth is hell, with everyone going to heaven.

What was the worldly life? The gay bright shimmering lunch, the many guests, the glitter of the table, mayonnaise red and green and yellow, delicate bright wines; strolling in the woods in the afternoon.... Tea, everyone telling anecdotes of the afternoon's walk as if it were a sort of competition, great bursts of laughter and abrupt silences and then another story, the moments of laughter were something like those moments in church; whilst there was nothing but laughter in the room everybody was perfectly happy and good; everybody forgot everything and ran back somewhere; to the beginning, to the time when they were first looking at things, without troubling about anything. But when the laughter ceased everyone ran away and the rest of their day together showed in a flash, an awful tunnel that would be filled with the echo of the separate footsteps unless more laughter could be made, to hide the sad helpless sounds. Dinners were like all the noise and laughter of tea-time grown steadier, a pillow fight with harder whacks and more time for the strokes, no bitterness, just buffeting and shouts, and everyone laughing the same laugh as if they were all in some high secret. They were in some high secret; the great secret of the worldly life; and if you prevented yourself from thinking and laughed, they seemed to take you in. That was the way to live the worldly life. To talk absurdly and laugh; to be lost in laughter. Why had Mrs. Corrie seemed so vexed? Why had she said suddenly and quietly in the billiard-room that it seemed rummy to go to Mass and play billiards in the evening? "*Be* goody if you *are*." It had spoiled the day. Mrs. Corrie would like her to be goody. But then it was she who had pushed her down the steps in the afternoon and called after the actor to take care of her in the woods.

There was something too sad about the worldliness and too difficult about goodness.

Perhaps one had not gone far enough with worldliness....

"Take each fair mask for what it shows itself,
Nor strive to look beneath it."

That was what she had done drifting about in the wood with the actor listening to his pleasant voice. It was an excursion into pure worldliness. He had never thought for a moment in his life of the world as anything than what it appeared to be. He had no suspicion that anyone ever did. He had accepted her as one of the house-party and talked, on and on busily, about his American tour and his hope of a London engagement, getting emphatic about his chance, the chanciness of everything. And she had drifted along, delighting in the pleasant voice sounding through the wood, seeing the wood clear and steady through the pleasant tone, not caring about chance or chanciness but ready to pretend she was interested in them so that the voice might go on; pretending to be interested when he stopped. That was feminine worldliness, pretending to be interested so that pleasant things might go on. Masculine worldliness was refusing to be interested so that it might go on doing things. Feminine worldliness then meant perpetual hard work and cheating and pretence at the door of a hidden garden, a lovely hidden garden. Masculine worldliness meant never being really there; always talking about things that had happened or making plans for things that might happen. There was nothing that could happen that was not in some way the same as anything else. Nobody was ever quite there, realising.

CHAPTER IV

1

During her second week of giving the children their morning's lessons Miriam saw finally that it was impossible and would always be impossible to make their two hours of application anything but an irrelevant interval in their lives. They came into the schoolroom with languid reluctance, dreamily indolent from breakfast in bed, fragrant from warm baths. They made no resistance. She sat with the appointed tasks clearly in mind, holding on to the certainty that they were to be done as the only means of getting through the morning. The excitement of taking up everything afresh with her was over and beyond occasional moments of brightness when she tried to impress a fact or lift them over a difficulty with a jest and they would exchange their glance of secret delight, their curious conspirators' glance of some great certainty shared, they went through their tasks with well-bred preoccupation, sighing deeply now and again and sometimes groaning, with clenched hands pressed between their knees. Their accustomed life of events was close round them, in the garden just beyond the undraped window, on the mat outside the schoolroom door, where at any moment a footstep crossing the landing might fall softly and pause, when their heads would go up in tense listening. "Rollo!" they would say, waiting for the turning of the handle, holding themselves in for the subdued shoutings they would utter when Mrs. Corrie appeared standing in the doorway with a finger on her lips. "Happy?" she would breathe; "working like nigger boys?" Unless Miriam looked gravely detached she would glide in blushing, and passionately caress them. When this happened, sighs and groanings filled the time that remained. Their nearest approach to open rebellion included a tacit appeal to her as a fellow-sufferer to throw up the stupid game. It was quite clear that they did not blame her for their sufferings and they were so much prepared to do the decent thing that her experiment of reading to them regularly at some convenient half-hour each day from a book of adventures or fairy tale, not only reconciled them to endure the morning's ordeal, but filled them with a gratitude that astonished her and the beginnings of a personal regard for her that shook her heart. During the readings they would lose their air of well-bred detachment and would come near. They would be relaxed and silent; the girl with bent head and brooding defiant curiously smiling and frowning face, the boy gazing at the reader, rapturous. She would sometimes feel against each arm the pressure of a head.

She had felt instinctively and at once that she could not use their lesson hours as opportunities for talking at large on general ideas as she had done with the children in the Banbury Park school. Those children, the children of tradesmen most of them, could be allowed to take up the beginnings of ideas; "ideals," the sense of modern reforms, they could be allowed to discuss anything from any point of view and take up attitudes and have opinions. The opportunity for discussion and for encouraging a definite attitude towards life was much greater in this quiet room with only the two children; but it would have been mean, Miriam felt, to take advantage of this opportunity; to be anything but strictly neutral and wary of generalisations. It would have been so easy. Probably a really "conscientious" woman would have done it, have "influenced" them, given the girl a bias in the direction of some life of devotion, hospital nursing or slum missionary work, and have filled the boy with ideas as to the essential superiority of "Radicals." Their minds were so soft and untouched.... It ended in a conspiracy, they all sat masquerading, and finished their morning exhausted and relieved. The children knew the lessons tortured her and made her ill at ease, and they were puzzled without disapproving. Through it all she felt their gratitude to her for not being "simple," like Bunnikin.

2

There was to be another week-end. Again there would be the sense of being a visitor amongst other visitors; visitor was not the word; there was a French word which described the thing, "convive," "les convives" ... people sitting easily about a table with flushed faces ... someone standing drunkenly up with eyes blazing with friendliness and a raised wineglass ... women and wine, the roses of Heliogabalus; but he was a Greek and dreadful in some way, convives were Latin, Roman; fountains, water flowing over marble, white-robed strong-faced people reclining on marble couches, feasting ... taking each fair mask for what it shows itself; that was what this kind of wealthy English people did, perhaps what all wealthy people did ... the maimed, the halt, the blind, *compel* them to come in ... but that was after the others had refused. The thing that made you feel jolliest and strongest was to forget the maimed, to *be* a fair mask, to keep everything else out and be a little circle of people knowing that everything was kept out. Suppose a skeleton walked in? Offer it a glass of wine. People have no right to be skeletons, or if they are to make a fuss about it. These people would be all the brighter if they happened to have neuralgia; some strong pain or emotion made you able to do things. Taking each fair mask was a fine grown-up game. Perhaps it could be kept up to the end? Perhaps *that* was the meaning of the man playing cards on his death-bed. Defying God. That was what Satan did. He was brave; defying a tyrant ... "nothing to do but curse God and die." Who said that? there was something silly about it; giving in, not real defiance. It didn't settle anything; if the new ideas were true; the thing went on. The love of God was like the love of a mother; always forgiving you, ready to die for you, always waiting for you to be good. Why? It was mean. The things one wanted one could not have if one were just tame and good.... It is morbid to think about being good; better the fair mask—anything. But it did not make people happy. These people were not happy. They were not real.

3

Spring; everywhere, inside and outside the house. The spring outside had a meaning here. It came in through the windows without obstruction and passed into everything. At home it had sent one nearly mad with joy and anticipation and passed and left you looking for it for the rest of the year; in Germany it had brought music and wild joy—the secret had passed from eye to eye; all the girls had known it. At Wordsworth House it had stood far away, like a picture in a dream, something that could be seen from windows, and found for a moment in the park, but powerless to get into the house. Here it came in; you could not forget it for a moment; and it was a background for something more wonderful than itself; something that made it wonderful; something there were no words for; voices, movements from room to room, strange food, the soft chink of Venetian glass, amber wine, the light drowned in wine, through the window a sharp gleam on things that reflected, day and night, into everything, even into one's thoughts. Why was the spring suddenly so real? Why was it that you could stand as it were in a shaft of it all the time, feeling in your breathing, hearing in your voice the sound of the spring, the blood in your fingertips seeming like the roses that they would touch soon in the garden?

How ignorant the man was who said, "each fair mask for what it shows itself." Life is not a mask, it is fair; the gold in one's hair is real.

4

Friday brought an atmosphere of expectation. Mr. Kronen, an old friend of the Corries, was coming down, with a new Mrs. Kronen.

By the early afternoon the house was full of fragrance; coming downstairs dressed for an errand in the little town two miles away, Miriam saw the hall all pink and saffron with azaleas. Coming across the hall she found a scent in the air that did not come from the azaleas, a sweet familiar syrupy distillation ... the blaze of childhood's garden was round her again, bright magic flowers in the sunlight, magic flowers, still there, nearer to her than ever in this happy house; she could almost hear the humming of the bees, and flung back the bead curtain with unseeing eyes half expecting some doorway to open on the remembered garden; the scent was overpowering ... the drawing-room was cool and silent with closed windows and drawn blinds; bowls of roses stood in every available place; she tiptoed about in the room gathering their scent.

As she opened the hall door Mrs. Corrie's voice startled her from the dining-room.

Going into the dining-room she found her with a flushed face and excited eyes and the children dancing round her. "Another tin! One more tin!" they exclaimed, plucking at Miriam. From the billiard-room came the smell of fresh varnish. Wiggerson was on her knees near the door.

"She's done some stupid thing," thought Miriam, looking at Mrs. Corrie's excited, unconscious face with sudden anxiety; "some womanish overdoing it, wanting to do too much and spoiling everything." She felt as if she were representing Mr. Corrie.

"Will it be dry in time?" she asked, half angrily, scarcely knowing what she said and in the midst of Mrs. Corrie's apologetic petition that she would bring a tin of oak stain back with her.

"Lordy, don't you think so?" whispered Mrs. Corrie, only half dismayed.

Miriam had not patience to follow her as she went to survey the floor ruefully chanting, "Oh, Wiggerson, Wiggerson."

"Anyhow I'm sure it oughtn't to have any more on as late as when I come back," she scolded boldly. How annoyed Mr. Corrie would be....

5

As she was going down the quiet road past the high oak garden palings of the nearest house she heard the bumping and scrabbling of a heavy body against the palings and a dog leapt into the road almost at her feet, making the dust fly. It was an Irish terrier. It smiled and barked a little, waiting, looking up into her face and up and down the road. "It thought it knew me," she pondered; "it mistook me for someone else." She patted its head and went forward thinking of the joyful scrabbling, its headlong determination. The dog jerked back its head with a wide smile, tore down the road and came back leaping and smiling. Something disappeared from the vista of the roadway as the dog rushed along it nosing after scents, looking round now and again, and now and again rushing back to greet her. It brought back the sense of the house and the strange gay life she had just left to go on her errand to the little unknown town. It wore a smart collar; it belonged to that life. People in it were never alone; when they went out there was always a dog with them. "It thinks I'm one of them." But it liked the wild; when they came out on to the common it rushed up a sandy pathway and disappeared amongst the gorse bushes. For a while Miriam hoped it would come back and kept looking about for it; then she gave it up and went ahead with the commons drifting slowly by on either side; she wished that the action of walking were not so jerky, that the expanses on either side might pass more smoothly and easily by: "that's why people drive," she thought; "you can only really see the country when you are not moving yourself." Standing still for a moment she looked across the open stretch to her left and smiled at it and went on again, walking more quickly; the soft beauty that had retreated to the horizon when the dog was with her was spreading back again across the whole expanse and coming towards her; she hurried on singing softly at random, "Scorn such a *foe* ... though I could fell thee at a blow, though I-i, cou-uld fe-ell thee-ee a-at a-a *blow*" ... people walking and thinking and fussing, people driving somewhere in victorias were always coming along the road, to them it was a sort of suburb, quite ordinary, the bit near home. But it was big enough to be full of waves and waves of something real, something cool and true and unchanging. Had anybody seen it, did the people who lived there know it? Did anybody know this strange thing? She almost ran; *my* "commons," she said. "I know how beautiful you are; if only I knew whether you know that I know. I know, I know," she said, "I shan't forget you." "True, true till death; bear it, oh wind, on thy lightning breath."

6

The sun was very warm; before she reached the end of the long road the sandy pathways were beginning to glare. There was the river and the little bridge and the first shop just beyond it, where her purchase was to be made. Its wood-work was very bright white; it had a seaside look. She stood still on the slight ascent of the bridge mopping her face and preparing to represent Mrs. Corrie in the shop. Scrambling up the shallow bank from the common came the yellow dog. "Oh, hooray—you duck," she breathed, patting the warm stubbly head and listening to his breathless snortings. A piano-organ broke into loud music in the little street. It was not a mysterious little town, there was nothing of the village about it. The white framed windows held things you would see in a Regent Street confectioner's; it was a special shop for the kind of people who lived here. Miriam felt for her three and six and asked for her pound of coffee creams with a bored air, wishing she knew the dog's name so that she could claim him familiarly. She contented herself with telling him to lie down in an angry whisper repeatedly, as the creams were being weighed. He stood panting and gazing at her wagging his stump. "'Ullo, Bushy," said the shopwoman languidly; the dog faced round panting more loudly. "There you are, Bush," she said, as the scales balanced, and flung the dog a chocolate wafer which he caught with a snap. Miriam gazed vaguely at the unfamiliar spectacle, angrily feeling that the shopwoman was observing her. "You're not going to take him through the town?" said the shopwoman severely.

"Oh, no," said Miriam nervously.

"He's the worst fighter in the parish; they never bring him into the town unless it's the groom sometimes."

"Thank you," said Miriam, taking her bag of coffee creams. "Dogs *are* a nuisance, aren't they?" she added, in an emphatically sympathetic tone, getting away through the swing door almost hating the yellow body that squeezed through at her side and stood eagerly facing towards the market-place waiting for her movements.

7

She hurried up over the bridge calling to the dog without looking round, listening fearfully for sounds of conflict with a brown collie she had caught sight of standing with head high and ears pricked, twenty yards down the street. The piano-organ jingled angrily. The dog came thoughtfully trotting over the bridge and ambled off across the common—safe. He might have been killed, or killed another dog; how cruel dogs were, without knowing better. She looked to the common asking consolation for her beating heart. The bag of creams was safe and heavy in her hand, the dog had gone, the little town was behind, it had hurt her; it was spoiled; she would never like it. It had done nothing but remind her that she was a helpless dingy little governess. She toiled along, feeling dreadfully tired; the sounds of her boot soles on the firm, sand-powdered road mocked her, telling her she must go on. If she could be quite sure of finding a kind woman, not a hard-featured woman with black and grey hair, like the shopwoman, but kind, knowing and understanding everything, in a large print apron with her sleeves rolled up to the elbows, living in a large cottage with a family, who would look at her and smile a quiet short certain smile, as if she had been waiting for her, and take her in and let her help and stay there for ever, she would put down the bag of coffee creams on the edge of the common and go straight across it to her; but there would not be a woman like that here; all that the women round here would think about her would be to wonder which of the families she belonged to. If a victoria came along and in it a delicate, lonely old gentleman who had a large empty house with deep quiet rooms and a large sunny garden with high walls and wanted someone to be about there singing and happy till he died she would go. He would drive away with her and shut her up in the quiet beautiful house, protecting her and keeping people off, and she would sing all day in the garden and the house and play to him and read sometimes aloud, and he would forget he was old and ill, and they would share the great secret, dying of happiness. Die of happiness. People ought to be able to die of happiness if they were able to admit how happy they were. If they admitted it aloud they would pass straight out of their bodies, alive; unhappiness was the same as death, not suffering; but letting suffering make you unhappy—curse God and die, curse life, that was letting life beat you; letting God beat you. God did not want that. No one admitted it. No one seemed to know anything about it. People just went on fussing.

The violent beating of her heart died down. The sun was behind her; the commons glowed. She must have been looking at them for some time because she could close her eyes and see exactly how they looked, all alive in steady colour, gleaming and fresh. The thumping and trilling of the distant piano-organ offered itself equally to everybody. It knew the secret and twirled and swept all the fussing away into a tune. Quietly the clock of the church in the little town struck four. She would be late for tea. The children would have tea with Mrs. Corrie. Wiggerson would make a fresh pot for her when she got in. There would be a little tray in her quiet room, a cup and saucer, the little sprigged silk tea-cosy, the "Human Document." It would be the beginning of the week-end. It would link her up again with the early afternoon, the rose-filled drawing-room, the excited dining-room, the smell of varnish from the billiard-room floor.

8

Mrs. Corrie and the children were dancing in a lingering patch of sunlight at the far end of the lawn as Miriam came up the drive with her chocolates. They waved and shouted to her, trumpeting questions through their hands. She held up the bag. "Go and have *tea*, you poor soul," sang Mrs. Corrie. How excited they were. In the flower-filled hall Stokes, muttering excitedly to herself, was lighting the fire. The crackling of wood came from the dining-room.

Wiggerson was swishing about in the dining-room clearing away tea.

9

Sitting in her low basket chair with her dismantled tea-tray at her side and a picture in her mind of the new Mrs. Kronen coming down from London in the train in bright new clothes and a dust-cloak, Miriam was startled by hearing frightened footsteps rush across the landing and a frightened voice calling for Wiggerson.

"Something's happened," she told herself angrily, "it always does when everybody's so excited—'tel qui rit vendredi dimanche pleurera.'"

Opening the door she found the landing empty and quiet, the setting sun streamed across its coloured spaces, the flowers blazed as if they were standing in a garden.... Joey always went for walks if she were feeling thick and fat, she always went for a long walk; in coats with skirts to match; a costume; never a jacket with a different skirt ... the long cool passage leading away to the invisible door of Mr. Corrie's room was full of wreathing smoke. Wiggerson rushed across the landing along the passage, followed by Mrs. Corrie, with her head up and her handkerchief to her nose and all her figure tense and angular and strong. Both had passed silently; but there were shriekings on the stairs and the children came at Miriam with cries and screams. "Rollo'll be *killed*"; "Go to her"; "Go and save vem"; the children shrieked and leaped up and down in front of her. The boy's white features worked as if they must dislocate; his eyes were black with terror; he wrung his hands. Sybil's face, scarlet and shapeless and streaming with tears, blazed wrath at Miriam through her green eyes. "Be quiet," Miriam said in loud tones. "I shall do nothing till you are quiet." With a shriek the girl lashed at her with the dog-whip. "Save vem, *save* vem," shrieked the boy, twisting his arms in the air. "Will you both be quiet *instantly*?" shouted Miriam, as the blood rose to her head, catching and holding the boy. Both children howled and choked; Sybil flung herself forward howling, and Miriam felt her teeth in her wrist. The smoke came pouring out of the little hidden room, coiling itself against the air of the passage like some fascinating silent inevitable grimace. Wiggerson's figure flying through it stirred it strangely, but it closed behind her and billowed horribly out towards Mrs. Corrie standing just clear of its advance with her handkerchief pressed to her face, quiet, not calling to Wiggerson, waiting where she had disappeared. Miriam could not move. Sybil's body hung fastened to her own with entwining limbs ... "a fight in the jungle," a tiger flung fixed like a leech against the breast of a screaming elephant ... the boy had the whip and was slashing at her legs through her thin dress and uttering piercing shrieks.

10

"Stokes is an idjut," said Mrs. Corrie, going gaily downstairs with the two exhausted white-faced children followed by Wiggerson flitting along with bloodshot blinking eyes.

Stokes, sullenly brooding, lighting Mr. Corrie's fire without putting back the register. What was it that made Stokes sullen and brooding so that the accident had happened and the smoke had come? Stokes had seen something, someone, like the fearful oncoming curving stare of the smoke. Mrs. Corrie and Wiggerson did not brood like that. They laughed and wept and snatched things out of danger. They had thin faces. Mrs. Corrie was alone, like an aspen shaking its leaves in windless air. She knew she was alone. Wiggerson ... Wiggerson was...? Making her toilet in the spring sunset Miriam saw all that time Wiggerson's tall body hurtling about in her small pantry, quickly selecting and packing things on a tray—her eyes glancing swiftly downwards as her foot caught, the swift bending of her body, the rip, rip as she tore the braiding from her skirt, her intent face as she threw it from her and swept sinuously upright, her undisturbed hands once more at their swift work.

11

What a strange photograph ... a woman in Grecian drapery seated on a stonework chair with a small harp on her knees, one hand limply tweaking the strings of her harp; her head thrown back, her eyes, hard and bright, staring up into the sky, "Inspiration" printed in ink on the white margin under the photograph. It was an Englishwoman, a large stiff square body, a coil of carefully crimped hair and a curled fringe, pretending. There were people who would say, "What a pretty photograph," and mean it ... the draperies and the attitude. How easy it was to take people in, just by acting. Not the real people. There were real people. Where were they? That horrid thing could get itself on to Mrs. Corrie's drawing-room table and sit there unbroken. All women were inspired in a way. It was true enough. But it was a secret. Men ought not to be told. They must find it out for themselves. To dress up and try to make it something to attract somebody. She was not a woman, she was a *woman* ... oh, curse it all. But men liked actresses. They liked being fooled.

Miriam looked closely at the photograph with hatred in her eyes. Why not the stone steps and the chair and the sense of sunlight; sunlit air? That would be enough. "You get in the way of the air, you *thing*," she muttered, and the woman's helpless unconscious sandalled feet reproached her. Voices were shouting to each other on the upper landing. It was Mrs. Kronen's photograph, of course. Miriam moved quickly away, ashamed of having stared. But it was too late; she had done a horrid thing again. She saw, as if it were in the room with her, the affair of the taking of the photograph, a cross face coming down from its pose to argue with the photographer, and then flung upwards again, waiting. And she had put or let someone put it, in a frame, at once on a strange drawing-room table. Perhaps her husband had put it there. But if he valued it he would hide and shelter it.... When we meet, she will know I have stared at her photograph.

Mrs. Kronen came suddenly in with Mrs. Corrie, talking in a rich deep thick voice that moved, with large intervals, up and down a long scale and yet produced a curious effect of toneless flatness, just as if she were speaking a narrow nasal Cockney. There was a Cockney sound somewhere in her voice. She began at once loudly praising everything in the room, hardly pausing when Miriam was introduced to her, and giving no sign of having seen her. If I were alone with her, thought Miriam, I should want to say "'Ullo, 'ow's yourself?" and grin. It would be the only thing one could genuinely do. Mrs. Corrie almost giggled at the end of each of Mrs. Kronen's exclamations, but she was very gay and animated and so was Mr. Corrie when he came in with Mr. Kronen. They all went in to dinner talking and laughing loudly. And they went on laughing and joking and talking loudly against each other through dinner.

<h1 style="text-align:center">12</h1>

Mr. and Mrs. Corrie looked thin and small and very young. Once or twice they laughed at the same moment and glanced at each other. Mr. Corrie's face was flushed. Mr. and Mrs. Kronen looked like brother and sister—only that she said South Africa as if it were a phrase in a tragic recitative from an oratorio and he as if it were something he had behind him that gave him a sort of advantage over everyone. It seemed to be all he had. They had both been in South Africa, travelling in bullock waggons blinded by the fierce light and choked with sand. It seemed to linger in the curious brickish look of their complexions and the hard yellow of their hair. The talk about South Africa lasted all dinnertime. It seemed to interest Mr. Corrie. His eyes gleamed strangely as he talked about I.D.B.'s. Everybody at the table said, "Illicit dahmond bah" at least once with a little thrill of the face. Why was it illicit to buy diamonds?—strange people out there in the glare buying gleaming stones from miners and this curious feeling about it all round the table, everybody with hot glinting excited eyes—and somebody, some man, a business man who had handed round diamonds like chocolates to his friends in his box at the opera, a Stock Exchange man in a frock-coat throwing himself into the sea somewhere between England and South Africa—ah, what a pity, worried to death, with an excited head. He wanted diamonds. And when Mr. Corrie handed Mrs. Kronen a dish of fruit and said, "A banana? A bite of a barnato?" they all laughed, so comfortably. Something illicit seemed to creep into the very pictures and flow over the walls. The poor man's body falling desperately into the sea. He could not endure his own excited eyes.

13

Early on Monday morning Miriam heard Mrs. Kronen singing in the bathroom. She tried not to listen and listened. The bold sound had come in through her open door when Stokes brought her breakfast tray. With it had come the smell of a downstairs breakfast, coffee, a curious fresh, sustaining odour of coffee and freshly frying rashers. There was coffee on her own tray this morning and a letter addressed to her in a bold unknown hand. She sipped her coffee at once and put the overwhelming letter aside on her blue coverlet. It was an overweight, something thrown in on the surface of the tide on which she had awakened in the soft fresh harmonies of rose and blue of her curtained room. It could wait. It had come out of the world for her; but she felt independent of it. It did not disturb her. Its overwhelming quality was in the fact that she had called it to her out of the world. It was as if she had herself addressed the large bold envelope. She left it. Her sipped coffee steered her into the tide of the downstairs life. There was breakfast downstairs, steaming coffee and entrée dishes for Mr. Corrie and the Kronens, and they were all going off by the early train.

"C'est si bon," sang Mrs. Kronen in a deep baritone, as Miriam drank her coffee; "de con-fon-dre en un, deu-eux bai-sers." She sang it out through the quiet upstairs rooms, she met with it the bustle of preparation downstairs. It was a world she lived in that made her able to carry off these things without being disturbed by them, a rosy secret world in which she lived secure. A richness at the heart of things. She was there. She possessed it with her large strong brick-red and rose-white frame and her strong yellow hair. Did she, really? At any rate she wanted to suggest that she did—that that secret richness was the heart of things. She flung out boldly that it was and that she was there, but a sort of soft horrible slurring flatness in her voice suggested evil, as if a sort of restless acceptance of something evil was the price of her carelessness. Perhaps that was how things were. Perhaps that was part of taking each fair mask for what it shows itself. She made everyone else seem cloudy and shrivelled and dim. Miriam took up the stupendous envelope and held its solid weight in her hand as Mrs. Kronen sang on. "All right," she said, and smiled at it, feeling daring and strong. Its arrival would have been quite different if Mrs. Kronen had not been there; this curious powerful independent morning in the rose-blue room would not have happened in the same way without Mrs. Kronen.... Live, don't worry.... I've always been worrying and bothering. I'm going to be like Mrs. Kronen; but quite different, because she hasn't the least idea how beautiful things really are. She doesn't know that everyone is living a beautiful strange life that has never been lived before. If she did she would not be ashamed of herself. Miriam gave a great sigh and smiled.

14

Her breakfast was a feast. Sitting back under the softly tinted canopy with the soft folds of the bed curtains hanging near on either side she stared at the bright light pouring in through the lattices. Her room was a great square of happy light ... happy, happy. She gathered up all the sadness she had ever known and flung it from her. All the dark things of the past flashed with a strange beauty as she flung them out. The light had been there all the time; but she had known it only at moments. Now she knew what she wanted. Bright mornings, beautiful bright rooms, a wilderness of beauty all round her all the time—at any cost. Any life that had not these things she would refuse.... Roses in her blood and gold in her hair ... it was something belonging to them, something that made them gleam. It was her right; even if they gleamed only for her. They gleamed, she knew it. Youth, the glory of youth. So strong. She had got herself into this beautiful life, found her way to it; she would stay in it for ever, work in it, make money and when she was old, have soft, pink curtains and fragrant things to remind her, as long as she could lift her hand. No more ugliness, no more schools or mean little houses. Luxuries, beautiful gleaming things ... a secret happy life.

She smiled securely, with her eyes, the strange happy smile that had come in the brougham....

15

How strong Mrs. Kronen was.... How huge and strong she had looked standing in the hall while Mr. Corrie said cruel laughing little things about the billiard-room floor.... "She'll paint Madonna lilies on the table next." ... Mrs. Kronen saying nothing, smiling more and more without moving her face, growing bigger and stronger and taller as Mr. Corrie grumbled and Mr. Kronen fidgeted, cross and disappointed by the hall fire and then suddenly lifting her head and singing, a great flourish of clear strong notes filling the hall and pealing up through the house as she swept into the drawing-room.

Singing song after song to her own loud accompaniment, great emphatic sweeps of song, so that everyone came and sat about in the room listening and waiting, the men staring at the back of her head as she sat at the piano. Waiting, for music—they did not know they were waiting for music, waiting for her to stop getting between them and the music. They admired her, her magnificent singing and waited, unsatisfied, in the sweetness of the lamp-lit flower-filled room that her music did not touch. She sang on and on and they all grew smaller and smaller in the great sea of sound, more and more hopelessly waiting.

16

And Mrs. Corrie had sat deep in her large chair, dead and drowned. Dead because of something she had never known. Dead in ignorance and living bravely on—her sweet thin voice rising above the gloom where she lay hid—a gloom where there were no thoughts. Nearly all women were like that, living in a gloom where there were no thoughts. If anyone could persuade her that she was alive she would do nothing but rush about and dance and sing ... how irritating that would be ... making men smile and trot about and look silly ... no room for ideas; except in smoking-rooms—and—laboratories.... She was a good woman; a God woman; the sweetness of her bones and her thin sweet voice of tears and laughter were of God. Everyone knew that and worshipped her. Men's ideas were devilish; clever and mean.... Was God a woman? Was God really irritating? No one could endure God really.... Men could not.... Women were of God in some way. That is what men could never forgive; the superiority of women.... "Perhaps I can't stand women because I'm a sort of horrid man."

Mrs. Kronen was a sort of man too. She was not perplexed. But she was a woman too—because she was not mean and petty and fussy as men are ... sitting tall and square at the piano with the square tall form of her husband standing ready to turn the pages—her strong baritone voice rolling out, "Ai-me-moi ... car ton charme-est étrange ... et-je-t'ai-me."

17

Recalling the song as she sat back in the alcove of her bed motionless, keeping the brightness of her room at its first intensity, Miriam remembered that it had brought her a moment when the flower-filled drawing-room had seemed to be lit, from within herself, a sudden light that had kept her very still and made the bowls of roses blaze with deepening colours. In her mind she had seen garden beyond garden of roses, sunlit, brighter and brighter and had made a rapturous prayer. She remembered the words ... God.... I'm not afraid of you. Look at the gardens ... and something had smiled through the lit gardens exultantly, and Mrs. Kronen's voice had raged through the room like a storm, "Ai-me-moi!..." and Mr. Corrie's eyes were strange and hard with shadows.... He knew, in some strange way men knew there were gardens everywhere, not always visible. Women did not seem to know....

The letter on her tray was a sort of response to her prayer.

CHAPTER V

1

It was quite a long letter—signed with a large "Bob" set crosswise. It began by asking her advice about a wedding present for Harriett and ended with the suggestion that she should meet him and help him to make a suitable selection. It was written from the British Chess Club, to her, because Bob Greville wanted to see her. Harriett's wedding present was only an excuse. She flung the envelope and the two sheets of notepaper, spread loose, on her blue coverlet and smiled into her cup as she finished her coffee. Old Bob did not know that he had clad her in armour. He wanted to meet her alone. They two people were to meet and talk, without any reason, because they wanted to. But what could she have to say to anyone who thought that Mrs. Caudle's Curtain Lectures, even a nice edition bound in calf, or How to be Happy though Married, suitable for a wedding present for Harriett, or for anybody? Still, they might write to each other. It was right that letters, secret letters, should be brought into her blue room in the morning with her breakfast. She dropped out of bed smiling and sniffed at the roses she had worn the day before, standing in a glass on her washstand, freshened, half faded, half fresh, intoxicating as she bent over them. She dressed, without drawing back her curtains, in the soft rose-blue light, singing Mrs. Kronen's song in an undertone.

2

At eleven o'clock Mrs. Corrie swept into the schoolroom. Miriam looked easily up at her from the dreamy thicket where she and the children had spent their hour, united and content, speaking in undertones, getting easily through books that had seemed tiresome and indifferent the day before. She had felt the play of her mind on theirs and their steady adult response. They had joined as conspirators in this mad contemptible business of mastering the trick of the text-book, each dreaming the while his own dream.

"You darlings," cried Mrs. Corrie, "how sweet you all look!" They raised drunken eyes and beamed drowsily at her. "Give them a holiday," said Mrs. Corrie, raising her hands over the table like a conductor about to start an orchestra. "Give them a holiday—a picnic—and come and buy hats!"

In a moment the room was in an uproar of capering figures. "Hats! A new hat for Rollo! Heaps of cash! I've got heaps of cash!"

Miriam blinked from her thicket. This was anarchy; she felt herself sliding. But they were so old. All so old and experienced. She so young, by so far the youngest of the four.

<h2 style="text-align:center">3</h2>

Mrs. Corrie sat back in the victoria, her face alight under the cream lace veil she had twisted round her soft winter hat, and talked in quiet clipped phrases: soft shouts. They were driving swiftly through the fresh warmth of the April midday.

They were off for the afternoon. The commons gleamed a prelude. Miriam saw that Mrs. Corrie did not notice them nor think of sweeping back across them later on through the afternoon air and seeing them move and gleam in the afternoon light. She did not think of the bright shops, the strangely dyed artificial flowers with their curious fascinating smell interwoven with the strange warm smell of velvet and chenille and straw.... Miriam had once bought a hat in a shop in Kensington. As long as it lasted it had kept for her whenever she looked at its softly dyed curiously plaited straw something of the exciting fascination of the shop, the curious faint flat odours of millinery, the peculiar dim warm smell of silks and velvets — silk, China and Japan, silkworms weaving shining threads in the dark. Even when it had become associated with outings and events and shabby with exposure it remained each time she took it afresh from its box of wrappings, a mysterious sacred thing; and the soft blending of its colours, the coiled restraint of its shape, the texture of its snuggled trimmings were a support, refreshing her thoughts. She had never known anyone who went regularly to good hatshops; the sense of them as a part of life was linked only with Mrs. Kronen — Mrs. Kronen's little close toque made of delicately shaded velvet violets and lined with satin, her silky peacock blue straw shining with rich filmy tones, its mass of dull shot blue-green ribbon and the soft rose pink of its velvet roses. These hats had excited Mrs. Corrie; the hats and the sand-coloured silk dust cloak explained her cheque and her sudden happiness. But they only made her want to buy hats. The going and the shops were nothing to her. She talked about the Kronens as they drove, speaking as though she wanted Miriam to hear without answering. "She knows Mrs. Kronen fascinates me," thought Miriam.

"Ain't they a pair, lordy ... him divorced and her divorced and then marryin' each other. Ain't it scandalous, eh?"

People like the Corries disapproved of people like the Kronens, but had them to stay with them and were excited about their clothes. Miriam returned to listen to the singing of her body; it would sing until they got to the station. As she listened she held firmly clasped the letter she had addressed to the British Chess Club to say she would be nowhere near London until the weddings. "She doesn't care a rap about him—not a teeny rap ... she's a wise lady ... dollars—that's the thing," whispered Mrs. Corrie gaily. What does she want me to say? thought Miriam. What would she say if I pretended to agree?

Should she tell her about the weddings? Perhaps not. It would be time enough, she reflected rapidly, when she had to ask permission to go home for them. Mrs. Corrie had not asked her a single question about things at home, and if she were to say, "We used to live in a big house and my father lost nearly all his money and we live now in a tiny villa and two of my sisters are to be married," it would break into this strange easy new life. It would break the charm and not bring her any nearer to Mrs. Corrie. And Mrs. Corrie would not really understand about the home troubles. Mrs. Corrie had always been lonely and sad, inside. She had been an orphan, but brought up by a wealthy uncle and always living in wealth and now she seemed to think about nothing but the children and the house and the garden—hating theatres and dances and never going to them or paying visits or seeing the wonder of anything. She would only say, "Don't you marry yourself off, young lady, marriage is a fraud. You wait for a wealthy one." Whatever one said to her, whatever joy one showed her would lead to that.

But the two weddings hovered about the commons. They were a great possession. Nothing to worry about in them. Gerald and Bennett who had managed everything since the smash would manage them. Sarah and Harriet would be married from the little villa and would be Mrs. Brodie and Mrs. Ducayne just like anybody else. So safe. And she herself, free, getting interesting letters, going up to town with Mrs. Corrie, no worry, spring hats and the commons and garden waiting for them. She was sure she did not want to see the commons overburdened by the idea of her own wedding. Two was enough for the present. Of course, some day—someone, somewhere, wonderful and different from everyone else. Cash—no, not business and cigars and offices ... the city, horrible bloated men with shapeless figures, horrible chemists' shops advertising pick-me-ups ... a cottage—a cottage. Why did people laugh at love in a cottage? The outsides of cottages were the best part, everyone said. They were dark inside; but why not? A lamp; and outside the garden and the light.

"She's had all *kinds* of operations," mused Mrs. Corrie.

"Really?"

"Deadly awful. In nursing homes. She'll never have any kiddies."

Were there cold shadows on everything, everywhere?

She turned a pleading face to Mrs. Corrie. They were driving into the station yard.

"It's true, true, true," laughed Mrs. Corrie. "She doesn't care, she doesn't want any. They're all like that, that sort."

Miriam mused intensely. She felt Mrs. Kronen ought to be there to answer. She had some secret Mrs. Corrie did not possess. Mrs. Corrie looked suddenly small and mild and funny. Why did she think it dreadful that Mrs. Kronen should have no children? There was nothing wonderful in having children. It was better to sing. She was perfectly sure that she herself did not want children.... "Superior women don't marry," she said, "sir she said, sir she said, su, per, i, or women" —but that meant blue stockings.

<h4 style="text-align:center">4</h4>

"I don't want a silly hat," said Mrs. Corrie, as their hansom drew up in bright sunlight outside a milliner's at the southern end of Regent Street. "Let's buy a real lovely teapot or a Bartolozzi or somethin'. What fun to go home with somethin' real nice. Eh? A real real beauty Dresden teapot," she chanted, floating into the dimness of the shop where large hats standing on long straight stands flared softly like blossoms in the twilight.

She swept about in her flowing lace-trimmed twine-coloured overcoat on the green velvet carpet, or stood ruthlessly trying on a hat, pressing its wire frame to fit her head, crushing her fingers into tucked tulle, talking and trying, and discarding until the collection was exhausted. Miriam sat angry and admiring, wondering at the subdued helplessness of the satin-clad assistant, sorry for the discarded hats lying carelessly about, their glory dimmed. All the hats, whatever their shape or colour seemed to her to decorate the bronze head and the twine-coloured coat. The little toques gave slenderness and willowy height, and the large flowered ribboned hats, the moment a veil draped the boniness of the face made, Miriam felt, an entrancing picturesqueness. With each hat Mrs. Corrie addressed the large mirror calling herself a freak, a sketch, a nightmare, a real real fogey.

<h4 style="text-align:center">5</h4>

The process seemed endless and Miriam sat at last scourging herself with angry questions. "Why doesn't she decide," she found herself repeating almost aloud, her hot tired eyes turning for relief to the soft guipure-edged tussore curtain screening the lower part of the window, "what kind of hat she really wants and then look at the few most like it and perhaps have one altered?..." "It's so awfully silly not to have a plan. She'll go on simply for ever." But the soft curtain running so evenly along its smooth clean brass rod was restful, and plan or no plan the trouble would presently come to an end and there would be no discomforts to face when it was over—no vulgar bun shops, no struggling on to a penny 'bus with your ride perhaps spoiled by a dreadful neighbour, but Regent Street in the bright sun, a hansom, a smart obliging driver with a buttonhole, skimming along to tea somewhere, the first-class journey home, the carriage at the station, the green commons.

"Perhaps," said the assistant at last in a cheerful suggestive furious voice, flinging aside with just Mrs. Corrie's cheerful abandon, a large cream lace hat with a soft fresh mass of tiny banksia roses under its left brim, "Perhaps moddom will allow me to make her a shape and trim it to her own design."

Mrs. Corrie stood arrested in the middle of the green velvet floor. Wearily Miriam faced the possibility of the development of this fresh opportunity for going on for ever.

"Wouldn't that be lovely?" said Mrs. Corrie, turning to her enthusiastically.

"Yes," said Miriam eagerly. Both women were facing her and she felt that anything would be better than their united contemplation of her brown stuff dress with its square sleeves and her brown straw hat with black ribbon and its yellow paper buttercups.

"Can't be did though," said Mrs. Corrie in a cold level voice, turning swiftly back to the hats massed in a confused heap on the mahogany slab. Standing over them and tweaking at one and another as she spoke she made a quiet little speech, indicating that such and such might do for the garden and such others for driving, some dozen altogether she finally ordered to be sent at once to an address in Brook Street where she would make her final selection whilst the messenger waited. "Have you got the address all right?" she wound up; "*so* kind of you." "Come along, you poor thing you look worn out," she cried to Miriam, without looking at her as she swept from the shop. She waved her sunshade at a passing hansom and as it drew sharply up with an exciting clatter near the curb she grasped Miriam's arm, "Shall we try Perrin's? It's only three doors up." Miriam glanced along and caught a glimpse of another hat shop. "Do you really want to?" she suggested reluctantly. "No! No! not a bit old spoil sport. Chum yong, jump in," laughed Mrs. Corrie.

"Oh, if you really want to," began Miriam, but Mrs. Corrie, singing out the address to the driver was putting her into the cab and showing her how to make an easy passage for the one who gets last into a hansom by slipping into the near corner. Her appreciation of this little manœuvre helped her over her contrition and she responded with gay insincerity to Mrs. Corrie's assurance of the fun they would have over the hats at Mrs. Kronen's.... Tea at Mrs. Kronen's then. How strange and alarming ... but she felt too tired to sustain a *tête-à-tête* at a smart tea shop. "After tea we'll drop into a china shop and get somethin' real nice," said Mrs. Corrie excitedly, as they bowled up Regent Street.

6

They found Mrs. Kronen in a mauve and white drawing-room, reclining on a mauve and white striped settee in a pale mauve tea gown. On a large low table a frail mauve tea service stood ready, and Mrs. Kronen rose tall to welcome them dropping on to the mauve carpet a little volume bound in pale green velvet. On a second low table were strawberries in a shallow wide bowl, a squat jug brimming with cream, dark wedding cake hiding a pewter plate, a silken bag unloosed, showing marvellous large various sweetmeats heavy against its silk lining. As Mrs. Kronen slurred her fingers across Miriam's hand she ordered the manservant who had dipped and gathered up the green velvet volume to ask for the tea-cakes.

7

Then this was "Society." To come so easily up from the Corries' beautiful home, via the West End hat shop to this wonderful West End flat and eat strawberries in April.... If only the home people could see. Her fatigue vanished. Secure from Mrs. Kronen's notice she sat in a mauve and white striped chair and contemplated her surroundings.

While they were waiting for the tea-cakes, Mrs. Kronen trailed about the mauve floor reciting her impressions of the weather. "So lovely," she intoned in her curious half-Cockney. "I almost—went—out. But I haven't. I—haven't—stirred. It is lovely inside on this sort of spring day—the *light*."

She paused and swept about. There *is* something about her, thought Miriam. It's true, the light inside on a clear spring day.... I never thought of that. It is somehow spring in here in the middle of London in some real way. Her blood leaped and sang as it had done driving across the commons; but even more sweetly and keenly. It wouldn't be, in a dingy room, even in the country.... It's an essence—something you feel in the right surroundings.... What chances these people have. They get the most out of everything. Get everything in advance and over and over again. They can go into the country any minute as well as have clear light rooms. Nothing is ever grubby. And London there, all round; London ... London was a soft, sea-like sound; a sound shutting in the spring. The spring gleamed and thrilled through everything in the pure bright room.... She hoped Mrs. Kronen would say no more about the light. Light, light, light. As the manservant brewed the tea and the silver teapot shone in the light as he moved it—silver and strange black splashes of light—caught and moving in the room. Drawing off her gloves she felt as if she could touch the flowing light.... Flowing in out of the dawn, moving and flowing and brooding and changing all day, in rooms. Mrs. Kronen was back on her settee sitting upright in her mauve gown, all strong soft curves. "That play of *Wilde's* ..." she said. Miriam shook at the name. "You ought not to miss it. He—has—such—*genius.*" *Wilde* ... *Wilde* ... a play in the spring—someone named Wilde. Wild spring. That was genius. There was something in the name.... "Never go to the theatre; never, never, never," Mrs. Corrie was saying, "too much of a bore." Genius ... genius is an infinite capacity for taking pains. Capacity. A silly definition; like a proverb—made up by somebody who wanted to explain.... Wylde, Wilde.... Spring.... Genius.

8

The little feast was over and Mrs. Kronen was puffing at a cigarette when the hats were announced. As the fine incense reached her Miriam regretted that she had not confessed to being a smoker. The suggestion of tobacco brought the charm of the afternoon to its height. When the magic of the scented cloud drew her eyes to Mrs. Kronen's face it was almost intolerable in its keenness. She gazed wondering whether Mrs. Kronen felt so nearly wild with happiness as she did herself.... Life what are you—what is life? she almost said aloud. The face was uplifted as it had been in the photograph, but with all the colour, the firm bows of gold hair, the colour in the face and strong white pillar of neck, the eyes closed instead of staring upwards and the rather full mouth flattened and drooping with its weight into a sort of tragic shapeliness—like some martyr ... that picture by Rossetti, Beata Beatrix, thought Miriam ... perfect reality. She liked Mrs. Kronen for smoking like that. She was not doing it for show. She would have smoked in the same way if she had been alone. She probably wished she was, as Mrs. Corrie did not smoke. How she must have hated missing her smokes at Newlands, unless she had smoked in her room.

"It's—a—mis-take," said Mrs. Kronen incredulously, in response to the man's announcement of the arrival of the hats. She waved her cigarette "imperiously," thought Miriam, "how she enjoys showing off" ... to and fro in time with her words. Mrs. Corrie rose laughing and explaining and apologising. Waving her cigarette about once more Mrs. Kronen ordered the hats to be brought in and her maid to be summoned, but retained her expression of vexed incredulity. She's simply longing for us to be off now, thought Miriam, and changed her opinion a few moments later when Mrs. Kronen, assuming on the settee the reclining position in which they had found her when they came in, disposed one by one of the hats as Mrs. Corrie and the maid freed them from their boxes and wrappings, with a little flourish of the cigarette and a few slow words.... "Im-poss-i-ble; not-in-key-with-your-lines; slightly *too ingénue*," etc.: to three or four she gave a grudging approval, whereupon Mrs. Corrie who was laughing and pouncing from box to box would stand upright and pace holding the favoured hat rakishly on her head. The selection was soon made and Miriam, whose weariness had returned with the millinery, was sent off to instruct the messenger that three hats had been selected and a bill might be sent to Brook Street in the morning.

As she was treating with the messenger in the little mauve and white hall, Mrs. Corrie came out and tapped her on the shoulder. Turning, Miriam found her smiling and mysterious. "We're going by the 5.30," she whispered. "Would you like to go for a walk for half an hour and come back *here*?"

"*Rather!*" said Miriam heartily, with a break in her voice and feeling utterly crushed. The beautiful clear room. She loved it and belonged to it. She was turned out. "All right," smiled Mrs. Corrie encouragingly and disappeared. Under the eyes of the messenger and the servants who were coming out of the boudoir laden with hat boxes, she got herself out through the door.

CHAPTER VI

1

The West End street ... grey buildings rising on either side, feeling away into the approaching distance—angles sharp against the sky ... softened angles of buildings against other buildings ... high moulded angles soft as crumb, with deep undershadows ... creepers fraying from balconies ... strips of window blossoms across the buildings, scarlet, yellow, high up; a confusion of lavender and white pouching out along a dipping sill ... a wash of green creeper up a white painted house front ... patches of shadow and bright light.... Sounds of visible near things streaked and scored with broken light as they moved, led off into untraced distant sounds ... chiming together.

2

Wide golden streaming Regent Street was quite near. Some near narrow street would lead into it.

3

Flags of pavement flowing along—smooth clean grey squares and oblongs, faintly polished, shaping and drawing away—sliding into each other.... I am part of the dense smooth clean paving stone ... sunlit; gleaming under dark winter rain; shining under warm sunlit rain, sending up a fresh stony smell ... always there ... dark and light ... dawn, stealing....

4

Life streamed up from the close dense stone. With every footstep she felt she could fly.

5

The little dignified high-built cut-through street, with its sudden walled-in church, swept round and opened into brightness and a clamour of central sounds ringing harshly up into the sky.

6

The pavement of heaven.

To walk along the radiant pavement of sunlit Regent Street forever.

7

She sped along looking at nothing. Shops passed by, bright endless caverns screened with glass ... the bright teeth of a grand piano running along the edge of its darkness, a cataract of light pouring down its raised lid; forests of hats; dresses, shining against darkness, bright headless crumpling stalks; sly, silky, ominous furs; metals, cold and clanging, brandishing the light; close prickling fire of jewels ... strange people who bought these things, touched and bought them.

8

She pulled up sharply in front of a window. The pavement round it was clear, allowing her to stand rooted where she had been walking, in the middle of the pavement, in the midst of the tide flowing from the clear window, a soft fresh tide of sunlit colours ... clear green glass shelves laden with shapes of fluted glass, glinting transparencies of mauve and amber and green, rose-pearl and milky blue, welded to a flowing tide, freshening and flowing through her blood, a sea rising and falling with her breathing.

9

The edge had gone from the keenness of the light. The street was a happy, sunny, simple street—small. She was vast. She could gather up the buildings in her arms and push them away, clearing the sky ... a strange darkling and she would sleep. She felt drowsy, a drowsiness in her brain and limbs and great strength, and hunger.

A clock told her she had been away from Brook Street ten minutes. Twenty minutes to spare. What should she do with her strength? Talk to someone or write ... Bob; where was Bob? Somewhere in the West End. She would write from the West End a note to him in the West End.

10

There were no cheap shops in Regent Street. She looked about. Across the way a little side street showing a small newspaper shop offered help.

11

Thoroughly frightened she hurried with clenched hands down the little mean street ready to give up her scheme at the first sight of an unfriendly eye. "We went through those *awful* side streets off the West End; I was *terrified*; I didn't know *where* he was driving us," Mrs. Poole had said about a cabman driving to the theatre ... and her face as she sat in her thick pink dress by the dining-room fire had been cunning and mean and full of terror. A small shop appeared close at hand, there were newspaper posters propped outside it and its window was full of fly-blown pipes, toilet requisites, stationery and odd-looking books. "Letters may be left here," said a dirty square of cardboard in the corner of the window. "That's all right," thought Miriam, "it's a sort of agency." She plunged into the gloomy interior. "*Yes!*" shouted a tall stout man with a red coarse face coming forward, as if she had asked something that had made him angry. "I want some notepaper, just a little, the smallest quantity you have and an envelope," said Miriam, quivering and panic-stricken in the hostile atmosphere. The man turned and whisked a small packet off a shelf, throwing it down on the counter before her. "One penny!" bellowed the man as she took it up. "Oh, thank you," murmured Miriam ingratiatingly putting down twopence. "Do you sell pencils?" The man's great fingers seemed an endless time wrenching a small metal-sheathed pencil from its card. The street outside would have closed in and swallowed her up forever if she did not quickly get away.

12

"Dear Mr. Greville," she wrote in a clear bold hand.... He won't expect me to have that kind of handwriting, like his own, but stronger. He'll admire it on the page and then hear a man's voice, Pater's voice talking behind it and not like it. Me. He'd be a little afraid of it. She felt her hard self standing there as she wrote, and shifted her feet a little, raising one heel from the ground, trying to feminise her attitude; but her hat was hard against her forehead, her clothes would not flow.... "Just imagine that I am in town—I could have helped you with your shopping if I had known I was coming...." The first page was half filled. She glanced at her neighbours, a woman on one side and a man on the other, both bending over telegram forms in a careless preoccupied way—wealthy, with expensive clothes with West End lines.... Regent Street was Salviati's. It was Liberty's and a music shop and the shop with the chickens. But most of all it was Salviati's. She feared the officials behind the long grating could see by the expression of her shoulders that she was a scrubby person who was breaking the rules by using one of the little compartments with its generosity of ink and pen and blotting paper, for letter writing. Someone was standing impatiently just behind her, waiting for her place. "Telle est la vie," she concluded with a flourish, "yours sincerely," and addressed the envelope in almost illegible scrawls. Guiltily she bought a stamp and dropped the letter with a darkening sense of guilt into the box. It fell with a little muffled plop that resounded through her as she hurried away towards Brook Street. She walked quickly, to make everything surrounding her move more quickly. London revelled and clamoured softly all round her; she strode her swiftest heightening its clamorous joy. The West End people, their clothes, their carriages and hansoms, their clean bright spring-filled houses, their restaurants and the theatres waiting for them this evening, their easy way with each other, the mysterious something behind their faces, was hers. She, too, now had a mysterious secret face—a West End life of her own....

CHAPTER VII

1

The next morning there was a letter from Bob containing a page of description of his dull afternoon at his club within half a mile of her. "Let me know, my dear girl," it went on, "whenever you escape from your gaolers, and do not suffer the thought of old Bob's making himself responsible for all the telegrams you may send to cloud your joyous young independence."

Miriam recoiled from the thought of a dull bored man looking to her for enlivenment of the moving coloured wonder of London and felt that Mr. and Mrs. Corrie were anything but gaolers. She was not sorry that she had missed the opportunity of seeing him. "Meanwhile write and tell me your thoughts," was the only sentence that had appealed to her in the letter; but she was sure she could not whole-heartedly offer her thoughts as entertainment to a man who spent his time feeling dull in a club. He's ... blasé, that's it, she reflected. Perhaps it would be better not to write again. He's not my sort a bit, she pondered with a sudden dim sense of his view of her as a dear girl. But she knew she wanted to retain him to decorate her breakfast tray with letters.

2

The following day Mrs. Corrie decided that she did not want to keep the hats. She would spend the money intended for them on sketching lessons. An artist should come once a week and teach them all to paint from Nature. This decision excited Miriam deeply, putting everything else out of her mind. It promised the satisfaction of a desire she had cherished with bitter hopelessness ever since her schooldays when every Friday had brought the necessity of choking down her longing to join the little crowd of girls who took "extras" and filed carelessly in to spend a magic afternoon amongst easels and casts in the large room. The old longing came leaping back higher than it had ever done before, making a curious eager smouldering in her chest—as Mrs. Corrie talked. An old sketch-book was brought out and Mrs. Corrie spent the morning making drawings of the heads of the children as they sat at lessons. The book was almost full of drawings of the children's heads. Besides the heads there were rough sketches of people Miriam did not know. The first half-dozen pages were covered with small outlines, hands, feet, eyes, thumbs; a few lines suggesting a body. These pages seemed full of life. But the sketches of the children and the unknown people, sitting posed, in profile, looking up, looking down, full face, quarter face, three-quarters, depressed her. Learning to draw did not seem worth while if this was the result. The early pages haunted her memory as she sat over the children's lessons. Feet, strange things stepping out, going through the world, running, dancing; the silent feet of people sitting in chairs pondering affairs of state. Eyes, looking at everything; looking at the astonishingness of everything.

3

"That's the half-crown Mrs. Corrie gave me for the cabman, and the shilling for my tea," said Miriam, handing the coins to her companion as they bowled over Waterloo Bridge. Seagulls were rising and dipping about the rim of the bridge and the sunlight lay upon the water and shimmered and flashed along the forms of the seagulls as they hovered and wheeled in the clear air. Miriam glanced at them through the little side window of the hansom with a remote keen part of her consciousness ... light flashing from the moving wing of a seagull, the blue water, the brilliant sky, the bite of sun-scorched air upon her cheek, the sound about her like the sound of the sea.... As she turned back to the shaded enclosure of the hansom these things shrivelled and vanished and left her dumb, helplessly poised between two worlds. This shabby part of London and the seaside bridge could make no terms with the man at her side, his soft grey suit, his soft grey felt hat, the graceful crook of his crossed knees, his gleaming spats, the glitter of the light upon patent leather shoes. He was gazing out ahead, with the look with which he had looked across Australia in his gold-digging days, weary until he got back to the West End, not talking because the cab made such a noise crossing the bridge. It was stupid of her to peer out of her window and get away to her own world like that. Nothing that we can ever say to each other can possibly interest us, she reflected. Why am I here? Her coins reassured her.

"Don't think about pence, dear girl," he said, in a voice that quavered a little against the noise of the cab, "when you're with old Bob." Without looking at her he gently closed her hand over the money.

"All right," she shouted, "we'll see, later on!"

The cab swept round into a street and the noise abated.

"When we've dropped those famous hats and rung the bell and run away we'll go on to Bumpus's and choose our book," he said, as if asserting themselves and their errand against the confusion through which they were driving.

"Mrs. Caudle's Curtain Lectures," thought Miriam, glancing with loathing at the pointed corner of the collar that stuck out across the three firm little folds under the clean-shaven chin.... How funny I am. I suppose I shall get through the afternoon somehow. We shall go to the bookshop and then have tea and then it will be time to go back.

"The cabman is to take the hats into the shop and leave them. Isn't it extraordinary?"

Bob laughed with a little fling of his head.

"The vagaries of the Fair, dear girl," he said presently, in a soft blurred tone.

That's one of his phrases, thought Miriam—that's old-fashioned politeness; courtliness. Behind it he's got some sort of mannish thought ... "the unaccountability of women" ... who can understand a woman—she doesn't even understand herself—thought he'd given up trying to make out. He's gone through life and got his own impressions; all utterly wrong ... talking about them with an air of wisdom to young men like Gerald ... my dear boy, a woman never knows her own mind. How utterly detestable mannishness is; so mighty and strong and comforting when you have been mewed up with women all your life, and then suddenly, in a second, far away, utterly imbecile and aggravating with a superior self-satisfied smile because a woman says one thing one minute and another the next. Men ought to be horsewhipped, all the grown men, all who have ever had that self-satisfied smile, all, all, horsewhipped until they apologise on their knees.

4

They sat in a curious oak settee, like a high-backed church pew. The waitress had cleared away the tea things and brought cigarettes, large flat Turkish cigarettes. Responding to her companion's elaborate apologetic petition for permission to smoke it did not occur to Miriam to confess that she herself occasionally smoked. She forgot the fact in the completeness of her contentment. On the square oak table in front of them was a bowl of garden anemones, mauve and scarlet with black centres, flaring richly in the soft light coming through the green-tinted diamond panes of a little low square deep-silled window. On either side of the window short red curtains were drawn back and hung in straight, close folds ... scarlet geraniums ...

against the creamy plaster wall. Bowls of flowers stood on other tables placed without crowding or confusion about the room and there was another green window with red curtains near a far-off corner. There were no other customers for the greater part of their time and when the waitress was not in the room it was still; a softly shaded stillness. Bob's low blurred voice had gone on and on undisturbingly, no questions about her life or her plans, just jokes, about the tea-service and everything they had had, making her laugh. Whenever she laughed, he laughed delightedly. All the time her eyes had wandered from the brilliant anemones across to the soft green window with its scarlet curtains.

CHAPTER VIII

1

When May came life lay round Miriam without a flaw. She seemed to have reached the summit of a hill up which she had been climbing ever since she came to Newlands. The weeks had been green lanes of experience, fresh and scented and balmy and free from lurking fears. Now the landscape lay open before her eyes, clear from horizon to horizon, sunlit and flawless, past and future. The present, within her hands, brought her, whenever she paused to consider it, to the tips of her toes, as if its pressure lifted her. She would push it off, smiling—turning and shutting herself away from it, with laughter and closed eyes, she found herself deeper in the airy flood and drawing breath swam forward.

The old troubles, the things she had known from the beginning, the general shadow that lay over the family life and closed punctually in whenever the sun began to shine, her own personal thoughts, the impossibility of living with people, poverty, disease, death in a dark corner, had moved and changed, melted and flowed away.

The family shadow had shrunk long ago, back in the winter months they had spent in Bennett's little bachelor villa, to a small black cloud of disgrace hanging over her father. At the time of its appearance, when the extent of his embarrassment was exactly known, she had sunk for a while under the conviction that the rest of her life must be spent in a vain attempt to pay off his debts. Her mind revolved round the problem hopelessly.... Even if she went on the stage she could not make enough to pay off one of his creditors. Most women who went on the stage, Gerald had said, made practically nothing, and the successful ones had to spend enormous sums in bribery whilst they were making their way—even the orchestra expected to be flattered and bribed. She would have to go on being a resident governess, keeping ten pounds a year for dress and paying over the rest of her salary. Her bitter rebellion against this prospect was reinforced by the creditors' refusal to make her father a bankrupt. The refusal brought her a picture of the creditors, men "on the Stock Exchange," sitting in a circle, in frock-coats, talking over her father's affairs. She winced, her blood came scorching against her skin. She confronted them, "Stop!" she shouted, "stop *talking*—you smug ugly men! You shall be paid. Stop! Go away...." But Gerald had said, "They *like* the old boy ... it won't hurt *them* ... they're all made of money." They liked him. They would be kind. What right had they to be "kind"? They would be kind to her too. They would smile at her plan of restitution and put it on one side. And yet secretly she knew that each one of them would like to be paid and was vexed and angry at losing money just as she was angry at having to sacrifice her life to them. She would not sacrifice her life, but if ever she found herself wealthy she would find out their names and pay them secretly. Probably that would be never.

Disgrace closed round her, stifling. "It's *us*—we're doomed," she thought, feeling the stigma of her family in her flesh. "If I go on after this, holding up my head, I shall be a liar and a cheat. It will show in my face and in my walk, always." She bowed her head. "I want to live," murmured something. "I want to live, even if I slink through life. I will. I don't care inside. I shall always have myself to be with."

Something that was not touched, that sang far away down inside the gloom, that cared nothing for the creditors and could get away down and down into the twilight far away from the everlasting accusations of humanity.... The disgrace sat only in the muscles of her face, in her muscles, the stuff of her that had defied and fought and been laughed at and beaten. It would not get deeper. Deeper down was something cool and fresh— endless—an endless garden. In happiness it came up and made everything in the world into a garden. Sorrow blotted it over, but it was always there, waiting and looking on. It had looked on in Germany and had loved the music and the words and the happiness of the German girls and at Banbury Park, giving her no peace until she got away.

And now it had come to the surface and was with her all the time. Away in the distance filling in the horizon was the home life. Beyond the horizon, gone away for ever into some outer darkness were her old ideas of trouble, disease and death. Once they had been always quite near at hand, always ready to strike, laying cold hands on everything. They would return, but they would be changed. No need to fear them any more. She had seen them change. And when at last they came back, when there was nothing else left in front of her they would still be changing. "Get along, old ghosts," she said, and they seemed friendly and smiling. Her father and mother, whose failure and death she had foreseen as a child with sudden bitter tears, were going on now step by step towards these ghostly things in the small bright lamplit villa in Gunnersbury. She had watched them there during the winter months before she came to Newlands. They had some secret together and did not feel the darkness. Their eyes were careless and bright. Startled, she had heard them laugh together as they talked in their room. Often their eyes were preoccupied, as if they were looking at a picture. She had laughed aloud at the thought whenever there had been any excuse, and they had always looked at her when she laughed her loud laugh. Had they understood? Did they know that it was themselves laughing in her? Families ought to laugh together whenever there was any excuse. She felt that her own grown-up laughter was the end of all the dreadful years. And three weeks ahead were the two weddings. The letters from home gleamed with descriptions of the increasing store of presents and new-made clothing. Miriam felt that they were her own; she would see them all at the last best moment when they were complete. She would have all that and all her pride in the outgoing lives of Sarah and Harriett that were like two sunlit streams. And meanwhile here within her hands was Newlands. Three weeks of days and nights of untroubled beauty. Interminable.

2

The roses were in bud. Every day she managed to visit them at least once, running out alone into the garden at twilight and coming back rich with the sense of the twilit green garden and the increasing stripes of colour between the tight shining green sheaths.

3

There had been no more talk of painting lessons. The idea had died in Mrs. Corrie's mind the day after it had been born and a strange interest, something dreadful that was happening in London had taken its place. It seemed to absorb her completely and to spread a strange curious excitement throughout the house. She sent a servant every afternoon up to the station for an evening newspaper. The pink papers disappeared, but she was perpetually making allusions to their strange secret in a way that told Miriam she wanted to impart it and that irritated without really arousing her interest. She felt that anything that was being fussed over in pink evening papers was probably really nothing at all. She could not believe that anything that had such a strange effect on Mrs. Corrie could really interest her. But she longed to know exactly what the mysterious thing was. If it was simply a divorce case Mrs. Corrie would have told her about it, dropping out the whole story abstractedly in one of her little shocked sentences and immediately going on to speak of something else. She did not want to hear anything more about divorce; all her interested curiosity in divorced people had been dispersed by her contact with the Kronens. They had both been divorced and their lives were broken and muddly and they were not sure of themselves. Mrs. Kronen was strong and alone. But she was alone and would always be. If it were a murder everybody would talk about it openly. It must be something worse than a murder or a divorce. She felt she must know, must make Mrs. Corrie tell her and knew at the same time that she did not want to be distracted from the pure solid glory of the weeks by sharing a horrible secret. The thing kept Mrs. Corrie occupied and interested and left her free to live undisturbed. It was a barrier between them. And yet ... something that a human being had done that was worse than a murder or a divorce.

"Is it a divorce?" she said suddenly and insincerely one afternoon coming upon Mrs. Corrie scanning the newly arrived newspaper in the garden.

"Lordy no," laughed Mrs. Corrie self-consciously, scrumpling the paper under her arm.

"What is it?" said Miriam, shaking and flushing. "Don't tell me, don't tell me," cried her mind, "don't mention it, you don't know yourself what it is. Nobody knows what anything is."

"I couldn't tell you!" cried Mrs. Corrie.

"Why *not*?" laughed Miriam.

"It's too awful," giggled Mrs. Corrie.

"Oh, you must tell me now you've begun."

"It's the most awful thing there is. It's like the Bible," said Mrs. Corrie, and fled into the house.

4

Little cities burning and flaring in a great plain until everything was consumed. Everything beginning again—clean. Would London be visited by destruction? Humanity was as bad now as in Bible days. It made one feel cold and sick. In the midst of the beauty and happiness of England—awful things, the worst things there were. What awful faces those people must have. It would be dreadful to see them.

5

At the week-end the house seemed full of little groups of conspirators, talking in corners, full of secret glee ... someone describing a room, drawn curtains and candlelight at midday ... wonderful ... and laughing. Why did they laugh? A candle-lit room in the midst of bright day ... wonderful, like a shrine.

The low-toned talk went on, in Mr. Corrie's little study behind the half-closed door, in corners of the hall. Names were mentioned—the name of the man who wrote the plays, Mrs. Kronen's "genius." Miriam could only recall when she was alone that it was a woodland springtime name. It comforted her to think that this name was concerned in the horrible mystery. Her sympathies veered vaguely out towards the patch of disgrace in London and her interest died down.

6

The general preoccupation and excitement seemed to destroy her link with the household. As soon as the children's tea was over she felt herself free. A strange tall woman came to stay in the house, trailing about in long jewelled dresses with a slight limp; Miss Tower, Mrs. Corrie called her Jin. But the name did not belong to her. Miriam could not think of any name that would belong to her ... talking to Mrs. Corrie at lunch with amused eyes and expressionless, small fine features of some illness that was going to kill her in eight or ten years, of her friends, talking about her men friends as if they were boys to be cried over. "Why don't you marry him?" Mrs. Corrie would say of one or another. How happy the man would be, thought Miriam, gazing into the strange eyes and daring her to marry anyone and alter the eyes. Miss Tower spoke to her now and again as if she had known her all her life. One day after lunch she suddenly said, "You ought to smile more often—you've got pretty teeth; but you forget about them. Don't forget about them"; and one evening she came into her room just as she was beginning to undress and stood by the fire and said, "Your evening dresses are all wrong. You should have them cut higher, above the collar-bone—or much lower—don't forget. Don't forget, you could be charming."

Mrs. Corrie came in herself the next evening and gave Miriam a full-length cabinet photograph of herself, suddenly. Afterwards she heard her saying to Kate on the landing, "Let the poor thing rest when she can," and they both went into Kate's room.

7

Every day as soon as the children's tea was over she fled to her room. The memory of Mrs. Corrie's little sketch-book had haunted her for days. She had bought a block and brushes, a small box of paints and a book on painting in water colours. For days she painted, secure in the feeling of Mrs.

Corrie and Kate occupied with each other. She filled sheet after sheet with swift efforts to recall Brighton skies—sunset, the red mass of the sun, the profile of the cliffs, the sky clear or full of heavy cloud, the darkness of the afternoon sea streaked by a path of gold, bird-specks, above the cliffs, above the sea. The painting was thick and confused, the objects blurred and ran into each other, the image of each recalled object came close before her eyes, shaking her with its sharp reality, her heart and hand shook as she contemplated it, and her body thrilled as she swept her brushes about. She found herself breathing heavily and deeply, sure each time of registering what she saw, sweeping rapidly on until the filled paper confronted her, a confused mass of shapeless images, leaving her angry and cold. Each day what she had done the day before thrilled her afresh and drove her on, and the time she spent in contemplation and hope became the heart of the days as April wore on.

8

On the last day of Jin Tower's visit, Miriam came in from the garden upon Mrs. Corrie sitting in the hall with her guest. Jin was going and was sorry that she was going. But Miriam saw that her gladness was as great as her sorrow. It always would be. Whatever happened to her. Mrs. Corrie was sitting at her side bent from the waist with her arms stretched out and hands clasped beyond her knees. Miriam was amazed to see how much Mrs. Corrie had been talking, and that she was treating Jin's departure as if it were a small crisis. There was a touch of soft heat and fussiness in the air. Mrs. Corrie's features were discomposed. They both glanced at her as she came across the hall and she smiled, awkwardly and half paused. Her mind was turned towards her vision of a great cliff in profile against a still sky with a deep sea brimming to its feet in a placid afterglow; the garden with its lawn and trees, its bushiness and its buttons of bright rosebuds had seemed small and troubled and talkative in comparison. In her slight pause she offered them her vision, but knew as she went on upstairs that her attitude had said, "I am the paid governess. You must not talk to me as you would to each other; I am an inferior and can never be an intimate." She was glad that Jin had left off coming to her room. She did not want intimacy with anyone if it meant that strained fussiness in the hall. Meeting Mrs. Corrie later on the landing she asked with a sudden sense of inspiration whether she might have her meal in her room, adding in an insincere effort at explanation that she wanted to do some reading up for the children. Mrs. Corrie agreed with an alacrity that gave her a vision of possible freedom ahead and a shock of apprehension. Perhaps she had not succeeded even so far as she thought in living the Newlands social life. She spent the evening writing to Eve, asking her if she remembered sea scenes at Weymouth and Brighton, pushing on and on weighed down by a sense of the urgency of finding out whether to Eve the registration and the recalling of her impressions was a thing that she must either do or lose hold of some essential thing ... she felt that Eve would somehow admire her own stormy emphasis but would not really understand how much it meant to her. She remembered Eve's comparison of the country round the Greens' house to Leader landscapes—pictures, and how delightful it had seemed to her that she had such things all round her to look at. But her thoughts of the great brow and downward sweep of cliff and the sea coming up to it was not a picture, it was a thing; her cheeks flared as she searched for a word—it was an experience, perhaps the most important thing in life—far in away from any "glad mask," a thing belonging to that strange inner life and independent of everybody. Perhaps it was a betrayal, a sort of fat noisy gossiping to speak of it even to Eve. "You'll think I'm *mad*," she concluded, "but I'm not."

When the letter was finished the Newlands life seemed very remote. She was alone in a strange, luxurious room that did not belong to her, lit by a hard electric light that had been put there by some hardworking mechanic to whom the house was just a house with electric fittings. She felt a touch of the half-numb half-feverish stupor that had been her daily mood at Banbury Park. She would go on teaching the Corrie children, but her evenings in future would be divided between unsuccessful efforts to put down her flaming or peaceful sunset scenes and to explain their importance to Eve.

CHAPTER IX

1

But the next evening when Mr. Corrie came down for the week-end with a party of guests, Mrs. Corrie appeared with swift suddenness in Miriam's room and glanced at her morning dress.

"I say, missy, you'll have to hurry up."

"Oh, I didn't dress ... the house is full of strangers."

"No, it isn't; there's Mélie and Tom ... Tommy and Mélie."

"Yes, but I know there are crowds."

She did not want to meet the Cravens again, and the strangers would turn out to be some sort of people saying certain sorts of things over and over again, and if she went down she would not be able to get away as soon as she knew all about them. She would be fixed; obliged to listen. When anyone spoke to her, grimacing as the patronised governess or saying what she thought and being hated for it.

"Crowds," she repeated, as Mrs. Corrie placed a large lump in the centre of the blaze.

They had her here, in this beautiful room and looked after her comfort as if she were a guest.

"Nonsensy-nonsense. You *must* come down and see the fun." Miriam glanced at her empty table. In the drawer hidden underneath the table-cover were her block and paints. Presently she could, if she held firm, be alone, in a grey space inside this alien room, cold and lonely and with the beginning of something ... dark painful beginning of something that could not come if people were there.... Downstairs, warmth and revelry.

"You *must* come down and see the fun," said Mrs. Corrie, getting up from the fire and trailing across the room with bent head. "A nun—a nun in amber satin," thought Miriam, surveying her back.

"*Want* you to come down," said Mrs. Corrie plaintively from the door. Cold air came in from the landing; the warmth of the room stirred to a strange vitality, the light glowed clearer within its ruby globe. The silvery clatter of entrée dishes came up from the hall.

"All right," said Miriam, turning exultantly to the chest of drawers.

"A victory over myself or some sort of treachery?" ... The long drawer which held her evening things seemed full of wonders. She dragged out a little home-made smocked blouse of pale blue nun's veiling that had seemed too dowdy for Newlands and put it on over her morning skirt. It shone upon her. Rapidly washing her hands, away from the glamour of the looking-glass, she mentally took stock of her hair, untouched since the morning, the amateur blouse, its crude clear blue hard against the harsh black skirt. Back again at the dressing-table as she dried her hands she found the miracle renewed. The figure that confronted her in the mirror was wrapped in some strange harmonising radiance. She looked at it for a moment as she would have looked at an unknown picture, in tranquil disinterested contemplation. The sound of the gong came softly into the room, bringing her no apprehensive contraction of nerves. She wove its lingering note into the imagined tinkling of an old melody from a wooden musical box. Opening the door before turning out her gas she found a small bunch of hothouse lilies of the valley lying on the writing-table.... Mrs. Corrie—"you must come."

2

Tucking them into her belt she went slowly downstairs, confused by a picture coming between her and her surroundings like a filmy lantern slide, of Portland Bill lying on a smooth sea in a clear afterglow....

"Quite a madonna," said Mrs. Staple-Craven querulously. She sat low in her chair, her round gold head on its short stalk standing firmly up from billowy frills of green silk ... "a fat water-lily," mused Miriam, and went wandering through the great steamy glass-houses at Kew, while the names that had been murmured during the introductions echoed irrelevantly in her brain.

"She *must* wear her host's colours sometimes," said Mr. Corrie quickly and gently.

Miriam glanced her surprise and smiled shyly in response to his shy smile. It was as if the faint radiance that she felt all round her had been outlined by a flashing blade. Mrs. Craven might go on resenting it; she could not touch it again. It steadied and concentrated; flowing from some inexhaustible inner centre, it did not get beyond the circle outlined by the flashing blade, but flowed back on her and out again and back until it seemed as if it must lift her to her feet. Her eyes caught the clear brow and smooth innocently sleeked dark hair of a man at the other end of the table—under the fine level brows was a loudly talking, busily eating face—all the noise of the world, and the brooding grieving unconscious brow above it. Everyone was talking. She glanced. The women showed no foreheads; but their faces were not noisy; they were like the brows of the men, except Mrs. Craven's. Her silent face was mouthing and complaining aloud all the time.

3

"Old Felix has secured himself the best partner," Miriam heard someone mutter as she made her fluke, a resounding little cannon and pocket in one stroke. Wandering after her ball she fought against the suggesting voice. It had come from one of the men moving about in the gloom surrounding the radiance cast by the green-shaded lamps upon the long green table. Faces moving in the upper darkness were indistinguishable. The white patch of Mrs. Corrie's face gleamed from the settee as she sat bent forward with her hands clasped in front of her knees. Beyond her, sitting back under the shadow of the mantelpiece and the marking board was Mrs. Craven, a faint mass of soft green and mealy white. All the other forms were standing or moving in the gloom; standing watchful and silent, the gleaming stems of their cues held in rest, shifting and moving and strolling with uncolliding ordered movements and little murmurs of commentary after the little drama—the sudden snap of the stroke breaking the stillness, the faint thundering roll of the single ball, the click of the concussion, the gentle angular explosion of pieces into a new relation and the breaking of the varying triangle as a ball rolled to its hidden destination held by all the eyes in the room until its rumbling pilgrimage ended out of sight in a soft thud. It was pure joy to Miriam to wander round the table after her ball, sheltered in the gloom, through an endless "grand chain" of undifferentiated figures that passed and repassed without awkwardness or the need for forced exchange; held together and separated by the ceremony of the game. Comments came after each stroke, words and sentences sped and smoothed and polished by the gloom like the easy talking of friends in a deep twilight; but between each stroke were vast intervals of untroubled silent intercourse. The competition of the men, the sense of the desire to win, that rose and strained in the room could not spoil this communion. After a stroke, pondering the balls while the room and the radiance and the darkness moved and flowed and the dim figures settled to a fresh miracle of grouping, it was joy to lean along the board to her ball, keeping punctual appointment with her partner whose jaunty little figure would appear in supporting opposition under the bright light, drawing at his cigarette with a puckering half-smile, awaiting her suggestion and ready with counsel. Doing her best to measure angles and regulate the force of her blow she struck careless little lifting strokes that made her feel as if she danced, and managed three more cannons and a pocket before her little break came to an end.

4

"It must be jolly to smoke in the in-between times," said Miriam, standing about at a loss during a long break by one of her opponents.

"Yes, you ought to learn to smoke," responded Mr. Corrie judicially. The quiet smile—the serene offer of companionship, the whole room troubled with the sense of the two parties, the men with whom she was linked in the joyous forward going strife of the game and the women on the sofa, suddenly grown monstrous in their opposition of clothes and kindliness and the fuss of distracting personal insincerities of voice and speech attempting to judge and condemn the roomful of quiet players, shouting aloud to her that she was a fool to be drawn in to talking to men seriously on their own level, a fool to parade about as if she really enjoyed their silly game. "I hate women and they've got to know it," she retorted with all her strength, hitting blindly out towards the sofa, feeling all the contrivances of toilet and coiffure fall in meaningless horrible detail under her blows.

"I do smoke," she said, leaving her partner's side and going boldly to the sofa corner. "Ragbags, bundles of pretence," she thought, as she confronted the women. They glanced up with cunning eyes. They looked small and cringing. She rushed on, sweeping them aside.... Who had made them so small and cheated, and for all their smiles so angry? What was it they wanted? What was it women wanted that always made them so angry?

"Would you mind if I *smoked*?" she asked in a clear gay tone, cutting herself from Mrs. Corrie with a wrench as she faced her glittering frightened eyes.

"Of *course* not, my dear lady—I don't mind, if you don't," she said, tweaking affectionately at Miriam's skirt. "Ain't she a gay dog, Mélie, ain't she a gay dog!"

5

"It's a pleasure to see you smoke," murmured Mr. Corrie fervently, "you're the first woman I've seen smoke *con amore*."

Contemplating the little screwed-up appreciative smile on the features of her partner, bunched to the lighting of his own cigarette, Miriam discharged a double stream of smoke violently through her nostrils—breaking out at last a public defiance of the freemasonry of women. "I suppose I'm a new woman—I've said I am now, anyhow," she reflected, wondering in the background of her determination how she would reconcile the rôle with her work as a children's governess. "I'm not in their crowd, anyhow; I despise their silly secret," she pursued, feeling out ahead towards some lonely solution of her difficulty that seemed to come shapelessly towards her, but surely—the happy weariness of conquest gave her a sense of some unknown strength in her.

For the rest of the evening the group in the sofa-corner presented her a frontage of fawning and flattery.

6

Coming down with the children to lunch the next day, Miriam found the room dark and chill in the bright midday. It was as if it were empty. But if it had been empty it would have been beautiful in the still light and tranquil. There was a dark cruel tide in the room, she sought in vain for a foothold. A loud busy voice was talking from Mr. Corrie's place at the head of the table. Mr. Staple-Craven, busy with cold words to hide the truth. He paused as the nursery trio came in and settled at the table and then shouted softly and suddenly at Mrs. Corrie, "What's Corrie having?"

"Biscuits," chirped Mrs. Corrie eagerly, "biscuits and sally in the study." She sat forward, gathering herself to disperse the gloom. But Mrs. Craven's deep voice drowned her unspoken gaieties ... ah—he's not gone away, thought Miriam rapidly, he's in the house....

"Best thing for biliousness," gonged Mrs. Craven, and Mr. Craven busily resumed.

"It's only the fisherman who knows anything, anything whatever about the silver stream. Necessarily. Necessarily. It is the—the *concentration*, the—the *absorption* of the passion that enables him to see. Er, the fisherman, the poet-tantamount; exchangeable terms. Fishing is, indeed one might say——"

The men of the party were devouring their food with the air of people just about to separate to fulfil urgent engagements. They bent and gobbled busily and cast smouldering glances about the table, as if with their eyes they would suggest important mysteries brooding above their animated muzzles.

Miriam's stricken eyes sought their foreheads for relief. Smooth brows and neatly brushed hair above; but the smooth motionless brows were ramparts of hate; pure murderous hate. That's men, she said, with a sudden flash of certainty, that's men as they are, when they are opposed, when they are real. All the rest is pretence. Her thoughts flashed forward to a final clear issue of opposition, with a husband. Just a cold blank hating forehead and neatly brushed hair above it. If a man doesn't understand or doesn't agree he's just a blank bony conceitedly thinking, absolutely condemning forehead, a face below, going on eating—and going off somewhere. Men are all hard angry bones; always thinking something, only one thing at a time and unless that is agreed to, they murder. My husband shan't kill me.... I'll shatter his conceited brow—*make* him see ... two sides to every question ... a million sides ... no questions, only sides ... always changing. Men argue, think they prove things; their foreheads recover—cool and calm. Damn them all—all men.

7

"Fee ought to be out here," said Mrs. Corrie, moving her basket chair to face away from the sun.

The garden blazed in the fresh warm air. But there was no happiness in it. Everything was lost and astray. The house-party had dispersed and disappeared. Mrs. Corrie sat and strolled about the garden, joyless, as if weighed down by some immovable oppression. If Mr. Corrie were to come out, and sit there too it would be worse. It was curious to think that the garden was his at all. He would come feebly out, looking ill and they would all sit, uneasy and afraid. But Mrs. Corrie wanted him to come out, knew he ought to be there. It was she who had thought of it. It was intolerable to think of his coming. Yet he had been "crazy mad" about her for five years. Five years and then this. Whose fault was it? His or hers? Or was marriage always like that? Perhaps that was why she and Mrs. Craven had laughed when they were asked whether marriage was a failure. Mrs. Craven had no children. Nothing to think about but stars and spirits and her food and baths and little silk dresses and Mr. Craven treated her as if she were a child he had got tired of petting. She did not even go fishing with him. She was lying down in her room and tea would be taken up to her. At least she thought of herself and seemed to enjoy life. But she was getting fatter and fatter. Mrs. Corrie did not want anything for herself, except for the fun of getting things. She cared only for the children and when they grew up they would have nothing to talk to her about. Sybil would have thoughts behind her ugly strong face. She would tell them to no one. The boy would adore her, until his wife whom he would adore came between them. So there was nothing for women in marriage and children. Because they had no thoughts. Their husbands grew to hate them because they had no thoughts. But if a woman had thoughts a man would not be "silly" about her for five years. And Mrs. Corrie had her garden. She would always have that, when he was not there.

"If you were to go and ask him," said Mrs. Corrie, brushing out her dress with her hands, "he'd come out."

"*Me!*" said Miriam in amazement.

"Yes, go on, my dear, you see; he'll come."

"But perhaps he doesn't want to," said Miriam, suddenly feeling that she was playing a familiar part in a novel and wanting to feel quite sure she was reading her rôle aright.

"You go and try," laughed Mrs. Corrie gently. "*Make* him come out."

"I'll tell him you wish him to come," said Miriam gravely, getting to her feet. "All *right*," she thought, "if I have more influence over him than you it's not my fault, not anybody's fault, but how horrid you must feel."

8

Miriam's trembling fingers gave a frightened fumbling tap at the study door. "Come in," said Mr. Corrie officially, and coughed a loose, wheezy cough. He was sitting by the fire in one of the huge armchairs and didn't look up as she entered. She stood with the door half closed behind her, fighting against her fear and the cold heavy impression of his dull grey dressing-gown and the grey rug over his knees.

"It's so lovely in the garden," she said, fervently fixing her eyes on the small white face, a little puffy under its grizzled hair. He looked stiffly in her direction.

"The sun is so warm," she went on hurriedly. "Mrs. Corrie thought——" she stopped. Of course the man was too ill to be worried. For, an eternity she stood, waiting. Mr. Corrie coughed his little cough and turned again to the fire. If only she could sit down in the other chair, saying nothing and just be there. He looked so unspeakably desolate. He hated being there, not able to play or work.

"I hate being ill," she said at last, "it always seems such waste of time." She knew she had borrowed that from someone and that it would only increase the man's impatience. "I always have to act and play parts," she thought angrily—and called impatiently to her everyday vision of him to dispel the obstructive figure in the armchair.

"Umph," said Mr. Corrie judicially.

"You could have a chair," she ventured, "and just sit quietly."

"No thanks, I'm not coming out." He turned a kind face in her direction without meeting her eyes.

"You have such a nice room," said Miriam vaguely, getting to the door.

"Do you like it?" It was his everyday voice, and Miriam stopped at the door without turning.

"It's so absolutely your own," she said.

Mr. Corrie laughed. "That's a strange definition of charm."

"I didn't say charming. I said your own."

Mr. Corrie laughed out. "Because it's mine it's nice, but it is, for the same reason, not charming."

"You're tying me up into something I haven't said. There's a fallacy in what you have just said, somewhere."

"You'll never be tied up in anything, mademoiselle—you'll tie other people up. But there was no fallacy."

"No verbal fallacy," said Miriam eagerly, "a fallacy of intention, deliberate misreading."

"No wonder you think the sun would do me good."

"How do you mean?"

"I'm such a miscreant."

"Oh no, you're not," said Miriam comfortingly, turning round. "I don't want you to come out"—she advanced boldly and stirred the fire. "I always like to be alone when I'm ill."

"That's better," said Mr. Corrie.

"Good-bye," breathed Miriam, getting rapidly to the door ... poor wretched man ... wanting quiet kindness.

"Thank you; good-bye," said Mr. Corrie gently.

9

"Then you'd say, Corrie," said Mr. Staple-Craven, as they all sat down to dinner on Sunday, evening ... now comes flattery, thought Miriam calmly—nothing mattered, the curtains were back, the light not yet gone from the garden and birds were fluting and chirruping out there on the lawn where she had played tennis all the afternoon—at home there was the same light in the little garden and Sarah and Harriett were there in happiness, she would see them soon and meantime, the wonder, the fresh rosebuds, this year's, under the clear soft lamplight.

"You'd say that no one was to blame for the accident."

"The cause of the accident was undoubtedly the signalman's sudden attack of illness."

Pause. "It sounds," thought Miriam, "as if he were reading from the Book of Judgment. It isn't true either. Perhaps a judgment can never be true." She pondered to the singing of her blood.

"In other words," said one of the younger men, in a narrow nasal sneering clever voice, "it was a purely accidental accident."

"Purely," gurgled Mr. Corrie, in a low, pleased tone.

"They think they're really beginning," mused Miriam, rousing herself.

"A genuine accident within the meaning of the act," blared Mr. Craven.

"An actident," murmured Mr. Corrie.

"In that case," said another man, "I mean since the man was discovered ill, not drunk, by a doctor in his box, all the elaborate legal proceedings would appear to be rather—superfluous."

"Not at all, not at all," said Mr. Corrie testily.

Miriam listened gladly to the anger in his voice, watching the faint movement of the window curtains and waiting for the justification of the law.

"The thing must be subject to a detailed inquiry before the man can be cleared."

"He might have felt ill before he took up his duties—you'd hardly get him to admit that."

"Lawyers can get people to admit anything," said Mr. Craven cheerfully, and broke the silence that followed his sally by a hooting monotonous recitative which he delivered, swaying right and left from his hips, "that is to say—they by beneficently pursuing unexpected—quite *unexpected* bypaths—suddenly confront—their—their examinees—with the truth—the Truth."

"It's quite a good point to suggest that the chap felt ill earlier in the day—that's one of the things you'd have to find out. You'd have, at any rate, to know all the circumstances of the seizure."

"Indigestible food," said Miriam, "or badly cooked food."

"Ah," said Mr. Corrie, his face clearing, "that's an excellent refinement."

"In that case the cause of the accident would be the cook."

Mr. Corrie laughed delightedly.

"I don't say that because I'm interested, but because I wanted to take sides with him," thought Miriam, "the others know that and resent it and now I'm interested."

"Perhaps," she said, feeling anxiously about the incriminated cook, "the real cause then would be a fault in her upbringing, I mean he may have lately married a young woman whose mother had not taught her cooking."

"Oh, you can't go back further than the cook," said Mr. Corrie finally.

"But the cause," she persisted, in a low, anxious voice, "is the sum total of all the circumstances."

"No, no," said Mr. Corrie impenetrably, with a hard face—"you can't take the thing back into the mists of the past."

He dropped her and took up a lead coming from a man at the other end of the table.

"Oh," thought Miriam coldly, appraising him with a glance, the slightly hollow temples, the small skull, a little flattened, the lack of height in the straight forehead, why had she not noticed that before?—the general stinginess of the head balancing the soft keen eyes and whimsical mouth—"that's you; you won't, you can't look at anything from the point of view of life as a whole"—she shivered and drew away from the whole spectacle and pageant of Newlands' life. It all had this behind it, a man, able to do and decide things who looked about like a ferret for small clever things, causes, immediate near causes that appeared to explain, and explained nothing and had nothing to do with anything. Her hot brain whirled back—signalmen, in bad little houses with bad cooking—tinned foods—they're a link—they bring all sorts of things into their signal boxes. They ought to bring the fewest possible dangerous things. Something ought to be done.

Lawyers were quite happy, pleased with themselves if they made some one person guilty—put their finger on him. "Can't go back into the mists of the past ... you *didn't understand*, you're not capable of understanding any real *movements* of thought. I always knew it. You think—in propositions. Can't go back. Of course you can go back, and round and up and everywhere. Things as a whole ... you understand nothing. We've done. That's you. Mr. Corrie—a leading Q.C. Heavens."

In that moment Miriam felt that she left Newlands for ever. She glanced at Mrs. Corrie and Mrs. Craven—bright beautiful coloured birds, fading slowly year by year in the stifling atmosphere, the hard brutal laughing complacent atmosphere of men's minds ... men's minds, staring at things, ignorantly, knowing "everything" in an irritating way and yet *ignorant*.

CHAPTER X

1

Coming home at ten o'clock in the morning, Miriam found the little villa standing quiet and empty in the sunshine. The sound of her coming down the empty tree-lined roadway had brought no face to either of the open windows. She stood on the short fresh grass in the small front garden looking up at the empty quiet windows. During her absence the dark winter villa had changed. It had become home. The little red brick façade glowed as she looked up at it. It belonged to her family. All through the spring weather they had been living behind the small bright house-front. It was they who had set those windows open and left them standing open to the spring air. They had gone out, of course; all of them; to be busy about the weddings. But inside was a place for her; things ready; a bed prepared where she would lie to-night in the darkness. The sun would come up to-morrow and be again on this green grass. She could come out on the grass in the morning.

2

The sounds of her knocking and ringing echoed through the house with a summery resonance. All the inside doors were standing open. Footsteps came and the door opened upon Mary. She had forgotten Mary and stood looking at her. Mary stood in her lilac print dress and little mob cap, filling the doorway in the full sunlight. She had shone through all the years in the grey basement kitchens at Barnes. Miriam had never before seen her face to face in the sunlight, her tawny red Somersetshire hair; the tawny freckles on the soft rose of her face; the red in her shy warm eyes. They both stood gazing. The strong sweet curve of Mary's bony chin moved her thoughtful mouth. "How nice you do look, Miss Mirry." Miriam took her by the arm and trundled her into the house. They moved into the little dining-room filled with a blaze of sunlight and smelling of leather and tobacco and fresh brown paper and string and into the dim small drawing-room at the back. The tiny greenhouse plastered on its hindmost wall was full of growing things. Mary dropped phrases, offering Miriam her share of the things that had happened while she had been away. She listened deferentially, her heart rising high. After all these years she and Mary were confessing their love to each other.

3

She went down the road with a bale of art muslin over her shoulder and carrying a small bronze table-lamp with a pink silk shade. The bright bunchy green heads of the little lopped acacia trees bobbed against their background of red brick villa as she walked ... little moving green lampshades for Harriett's life; they were like Harriett; like her delicate laughter and absurdity. The sounds of the footsteps of passers-by made her rejoice more keenly in her burdens. She felt herself a procession of sacred emblems, in the sunshine. The sunshine streamed about her from an immense height of blue sky. The sky had never been so high as it was above Harriett's green acacias. It had gone soaring up to-day for them all; their sky.

That eldest Wheeler girl, going off to India, to marry a divorced man. Julia seemed to think it did not matter if she were happy. How could she be happy?... Coming home from the "Second Mrs. Tanqueray" Bennett had asked Sarah if she would have married a man with a past ... it was not only that his studies had kept him straight. It was himself ... and Gerald too. It was ... there were two kinds of men. You could tell them at a glance. Life was clean and fresh for Sarah and Harriett.... There were two kinds of people. Most of the people who were going about ought to be shut up, somehow, in prison.

4

Eve came into the little room with her arms full of Japanese anemones. Behind her came a tall man with red-brown hair, a stout fresh face and beautifully cut clothes. Miriam bowed him a greeting without waiting for introduction and went on arranging her festoons of art muslin about the white wooden mantelpiece. He was carrying a trayful of little fluted green glasses each half filled with water. He came into the room on a holiday—a little interval in his man's life—delighted to be arranging the tray of glasses; half contemptuous and very happy. Pleased and surprised at himself and ready for miracles. He was not married—but he was a marrying man—a ladies' man—a man of the world—something like Bob Greville—with the same sort of attitude towards women.... "The vagaries of the Fair" ... a special manner for women and a clubby life of his own, with men. Women meant sex to him, the reproduction of the species my dear chap, and his comforts and a little music on Sunday afternoon. He loved his mother, that was certain, Miriam felt, from something in his voice, and respected all mothers; the sort of man who would "look after" a woman properly, but would never know anything about her. And there was something in himself that he knew nothing about. Some woman would live with him in loneliness, maddened, waiting for that something to speak. Secretly he would be half contemptuous, half afraid of her and would keep on always with that mocking, obsequious, patronising manner. Horrible—and so easy to deceive, and yet cruel to deceive. *Hit* him ... hit him awake. He put down the tray of glasses near the heap of anemones that Eve had flung on the table and enquired whether they were to put one bloom in each glass.... He had a secret, indulgent life of his own. Did he imagine that no one knew?... Eve giggled and tittered ... this new giggling way of Eve's ... perhaps it was the way the Greens treated young men; arch and silly, like the girls at the tennis club. He must see through it. He was not in the least like the tennis club young men, most of whom needed to be giggled at before they could be anything but just sneery and silly.

5

But it was fascinating, like something in a novel come true; the latest tableau in all the wedding tableaux; their own. Bennett and Gerald had swept the lonely Henderson family into this. One was going to be a sister-in-law for certain, to-morrow.... Held up by this dignity Miriam concentrated on her folds and loops, adjusting and pinning with her back to the room, listening to the sparring and giggling, the sounds of the tinkling glasses—the scissors snipping and dropping with a rattle on to the table, the soft flurring of shifted blossoms. The moment was coming. The man was being impudently patronising to Eve, but really talking at her, trying to make her turn round. She did not want him. There was something ... some quality in men that this kind of man did not possess ... something she knew ... who? It was somewhere, but not in him. Still, his being there gave an edge to her freedom and happiness. She owed him some kind of truth ... some blow or shock. Holding her last festoon in place she consulted some jumbled memory and found a phrase: "Will you people leave off squabbling and just see if this is all right before I nail it up?" She spoke in a cool even tone that filled the room. It startled her, making her feel sad, small and guilty. Still with her back to the room she waited during the moment of silence that followed her words. "It's simply lovely, Mirry," said Eve. Had she been more vulgar than Eve? She knew her decoration was all right and did not want an opinion. She wanted to crush the man's behaviour, trample on it and fling it out of the room. Eve was sweeter and more lovable than she. Mother said it was natural and right to laugh and joke with young men. No ... no ... no....

She glanced, asking Eve to hold the corner while she went for the hammer and nails. Eve came eagerly forward. The man was standing upright and motionless by the table, looking quietly at her as she stood back for Eve to substitute a supporting hand. "Er—let me do that," he said gravely—"or go for the hammer." He was at the door: "Oh—thanks," said Miriam, in a hard tone; "you will find it in the kitchen."

Eve remained holding the muslin with downcast face and conscious lips. Seizing a vase of anemones Miriam put it on the marble, bunching up the muslin to hide the vase.

"This is their smoking-room," she said, her voice praying for tolerance. Eve beamed sadly and gladly. "Yes—isn't it jolly?" Joining hands they waltzed about the room. Eve did not really mind; she fought, but there was something in her that did not mind.

6

Through the French windows of the new drawing-room Miriam saw a group of figures moving towards the end of the garden. In a moment they would have reached the low brick wall at the end of the garden. They might stand talking there with their heads outlined against the green painted trellis-work that ran along the top of the wall or they might walk back towards the house and see her at the window.

She hid herself from view. The room closed round her. She could not sit down on one of the new chairs. The room was too full. Things were speaking to her. Their challenge had sent her to the window when she came into the room. It had made her feel like a trespasser. Now she was caught. She stood breathing in curious odours; faint odours of new wood and fresh upholstery, and the strange strong subdued emanation coming from the black grand piano, a mingling of the smell of aromatic wood with the hard raw bitter tang of metal and the muffled woolly pungency of new felting.

The whole of the floor space up to the edge of the skirting was filled by a soft thick rich carpet of clear green with a border and centre-piece of large soft fresh pink full-blown roses. Standing about on it were a set of little delicate shiny black chairs, with seats covered with silken stripings of pink and green, two great padded easy-chairs, deep cushioned and low-seated, and three little polished black tables of different shapes. A black overmantel with shelves and side brackets, holding fluted white bowls framed a long strip of deeply bevelled mirror. The wooden mantelpiece was draped at the sides like the high French windows with soft straight hanging green silk curtains. At the windows long creamy net curtains hung, pulled in narrow straight folds just within the silk ones.

The walls swept up dimly striped with rose and green, the green misty and changeful, glossy or dull as you moved. And on the widest spaced wall dreadful presences ... two long narrow dark-framed pictures, safe and far-off and dreamy in shop windows, but now, shut in here, suddenly full of sad heavy dreadful meaning. A girl, listening to the words she had waited for, not seeing the youth who is gazing at her, not even thinking of him, but seeing suddenly everything opening far far away, and leaving him, going on alone, to things he will never see, joining the lonely women of the past, feeling her old self still there, wanting everyone to know that she was still there, and cut off, for ever. There was something ahead; but she could not take him with her. He would see it now and again, in her face, but would never understand. And the other picture; the girl grown into a woman; just married, her face veiled forever, her eyes closed; sinking into the tide, his strong frame near her the only reality; blindly trying to get back to him across the tide of separation.

Their child will come—throwing even the support of him off and away, making her monstrous ... and then born into life between them, forever, "drawing them together," showing they were separate; between them, forever. There was no getting away from that.

The strange strong crude odours breathing quietly out from the open lid of the new piano seemed to support them, to make them more mockingly inexorable.

7

The smell of the piano would go on being there while inexorable things happened.

Voices were sounding in the garden....

Hanging on either side of the mantelpiece were two more pictures—square green garden scenes.... There was relief in the deeps of the gardens and in under the huge spreading trees that nearly filled the sky. There were tiresome people fussing in the foreground ... Marcus Stone people—having scenes—not noticing the garden; getting in the way of the garden. But the garden was there, blazing, filled with some particular time of day, always being filled with different times of day.

There would be in-between times for Harriett—her own times. Times when she would be at peace in this room near the garden. Away from the kitchen and strange-eyed servants, and from the stern brown and yellow pig-skin dining-room. In here she would have fragrant little teas; and talk as if none of those other things existed. There were figures standing at the French window.

8

She opened the window upon Harriett and Gerald. Standing a little aloof from them was a man. As Harriett spoke to her Miriam met his strange eyes wide and dark, unseeing; no, glaring at things that did not interest him ... desperate, playing a part. His thin squarish frame hung loosely, whipped and beaten, within his dark clothes.

His eyes passed expressionlessly from her face to Harriett.

A great gust of laughter sounded from the open kitchen window away to the left, screened by a trellis over which the lavish trailings of a creeper made a bright green curtain. It was Bennett's voice. He had just accomplished something or other.

"Ullo," said Harriett. The strange man was holding his lower lip in with his teeth, as if in horror or pain.... They stood in a row on the gravel.

"Let me introduce Mr. Grove," said Harriett, with a shy movement of her head and shoulders, keeping her hands clasped. Her face was all broken up. She could either laugh or cry. But there was something, a sort of light, chiselling it, holding everything back.

Miriam bowed. "What's Bennett doing?" she said hurriedly.

"The last time *I* saw him he was standing on the kitchen table fighting with the gas bracket," said Gerald.

The sallow man drew in his breath sharply and stood aside, staring down the garden. Miriam glanced at him, wondering. He was not criticising Gerald. It was something else.

"I say, Mirry, what did you do to old Tremayne this morning?" went on Gerald.

"What do you mean?" said Miriam interested. This was the novel going on....

She must read it through even at this strange moment ... this moment was the right setting to read through Gerald that little exciting far-away finished thing of the morning, to know that it had been right. She felt decked. Gerald stood confronting her and spoke low, fingering the anemones in her belt. The others were talking. Harriett in high short laughing sentences, the man gasping and moaning his replies, making jerky movements. He was not considering his words, but looking for the right, appropriate things to say. Miriam rejoiced over him as she smiled encouragingly at Gerald.

"Well, my dear, he wanted to know—*who* you were; and he swears he's going to be engaged to you before the year is out."

"What abominable cheek," said Miriam, flushing with delight. Then she had taken the right line. How easy. This was how things happened.

"No, my dear, he didn't mean to be cheeky."

"I call it the most abominable cheek."

"No you don't"; Gerald was looking at her with fatherly solicitude. "That's what he said anyhow—and he meant it. Ask Harry."

"Frivolous young man."

"Well, he's an awful flirt, I warn you; but he's struck this time—all of a heap ... came and raved about you the minute he'd seen you, and when he heard you were Harry's sister that's what he said."

"I'm sure I'm awfully obliged to his majesty."

Gerald laughed and turned, looking for Harriett and moving to her. Miriam caught at a vision of the well-appointed man, a year ... a home full of fresh new things, no more need to make money; a stylish contented devoted sort of man, who knew nothing about one. It would be a fraud, unfair to him ... so easy to pretend to admire him ... well, there it was ... an offer of freedom ... that was admirable, in almost any man, the power to lift one out into freedom. He wanted to lift her out—her, not any other woman. It was rather wonderful, and appealing. She hung over his moment of certainty in pride and triumph. But there was something wrong somewhere; though she felt that someone had placed a jewel in her hair. Gerald had drawn Harriett through the doorway into the drawing-room. The sunlight followed them. They looked solid and powerful. The strange terrors of the room were challenged by their sunlit figures.

9

Moving to the side of Gerald's strange friend Miriam said something about the garden in a determined manner. He drew a sawing breath without answering. They walked down the short garden. It moved about them in an intensity of afternoon colour. He did not know it was there; there was something between him and the little coloured garden. He walked with bent head, his head dipping from his shoulders with a little bob at each step. Miriam wanted to make him feel the garden moving round them; either she must do that or ask him why he was suffering. He walked responsively, as if they were talking. He was feeling some sort of reprieve ... perhaps the afternoon had bored him. They had turned and were walking back towards the house. If they reached it without speaking, they would not have courage to go down the garden again. She could not relinquish the strange painful comradeship so soon. They must go on expressing their relief at being together; anything she might say would destroy that. She wanted to take him by the arm and groan ... on Harriett's wedding-eve, and when she was feeling so happy and triumphant....

"Have you known Gerald long?" she said, as they reached the house. He turned sharply to face the garden again.

"Oh, for a very great number of years," he said quickly, "a—very—great—number." His voice was the voice of the ritualistic curate at All Saints. He sighed impatiently. What was it he was waiting for her to say? Nothing perhaps. This busy walking was a way of finishing his visit without having to try to talk to anybody.

"How different people are," she said airily.

"I'm very different," he said, with his rasping, indrawn breath. A darkness coming from him enfolded her.

"Are you?" she said insincerely. Her eyes consulted the flowered border. She saw it as he saw it, just a flowered border, meaningless.

"You cannot possibly imagine what I am."

Her mind leapt out to the moving garden, recapturing it scornfully. He is conceited about his difficulties and differences. He doesn't think about mine. But he couldn't talk like this unless he knew I were different. He knows it, but is not thinking about me.

"Don't you think people are all alike, really?" she said impatiently.

"Our common humanity," he said bitingly.

She had lost a thread. They were divided. She felt stiffly about for a conventional phrase.

"I expect that most men are the average manly man with the average manly faults." She had read that somewhere. It was sly and wrong, written by somebody who wanted to flatter.

"It is wonderful, *wonderful* that you should say that to me." He stared at the grass with angry eyes. His mouth smiled. His teeth were large and even. They seemed to smile by themselves. The dark, flexible lips curled about them in an unwilling grimace.

"He's in some horrible pit," thought Miriam, shrinking from the sight of the desolate garden.

"What are you going to do in life?" she said suddenly.

During the long silent interval she had felt a growing longing to hurt him in some way.

"If I had my will—if—I had my will—I should escape from the world."

"What would you do?"

"I should join a brotherhood."

"Oh...."

"That is the life I should choose."

"Do you see how unfair everything is?"

"Um?"

"If a woman joins an order she must confess to a man."

"Yes," he said indifferently.... "I can't carry out my wish, I can't carry out my dearest wish."

"You have a dearest wish; that is a good deal."

She ought to ask him why not and what he was going to do. But what did it matter? He was going unwillingly along some dreary path. There was some weak helplessness about him. He would always have a grievance and be sorry for himself ... self-pity. She remained silent.

"I'm training for the Bar," he murmured, staring away across the neighbouring gardens.

"Why—in Heaven's name?"

"I have no choice."

"But it's absurd. You are almost a priest."

"The Bar. That is my bourne."

"Lawyers are the most ignorant, awful people."

"I cannot claim superiority." He laughed bitterly.

"But you can; you are. You can never be a lawyer."

"It is necessary to do one's duty. Occupation does not matter."

"There you are; you're a Jesuit already," said Miriam angrily, seeing the figure at her side shrouded in a habit, wrapped in tranquillity, pacing along a cloister, lost to her. But if he stayed in the world and became a lawyer he would be equally lost to her.

"I have been ... *mad*," he muttered; "a madman ... nothing but the cloister can give me peace—nothing but the cloister."

"I don't know. It seems like running away."

"Running towards, running towards——"

Can't you be at peace now, in this garden? ran her thoughts. I don't condemn you for anything. Why can't we stop worrying at things and be at peace? If I were beautiful I could make you be at peace—perhaps. But it would be a trick. Only real religion can help you. I can't do anything. You are religious. I must keep still and quiet....

If some cleansing fire could come and consume them both ... flaring into the garden and consuming them both, together. Neither of them were wanted in the world. No one would ever want either of them. Then why could they not want each other? He did not wish it. Salvation. He wanted salvation—for himself.

"My people must be considered first," he said speculatively.

"*They* want you to be a barrister. That's the last reason in the world that would affect *me*."

He glanced at her with far-off speculative eyes, his upper lip drawn terribly back from his teeth.

"He is thinking I am a hard unfeminine ill-bred woman."

"I do it as an atonement."

The word rang in the garden ... the low tone of a bell. Her thoughts leaned towards the strength at her side.

"Oh, that's grand," she said hastily, and fluted quickly on, wondering where the inspiration had come from: "Luther said it's much more difficult to live in the world than in a cell."

"I am glad I have met you, glad I have met you," he said, in a clear light tone.

She felt she knew the quality of the family voice, the way he had spoken as a lad, before his troubles came, his own voice easy and sincere. The flowers shone firm and steady on their stalks.

She laughed and rushed on into cheerful words, but his harsh voice drowned hers. "You have put my life in a nutshell."

"How uncomfortable for you," she giggled excitedly.

He laughed with a dip of the head obsequiously. There was a catch of mirth in his tone.

Miriam laughed and laughed, laughing out fully in relief. He turned towards her a young lit face, protesting and insisting. She wanted to wash it, with soap, to clear away a faint greasiness and do something with the lank, despairing hair.

"You have come at the right instant, and shown me wisdom. You are wonderful."

She recoiled. She did not really want to help him. She wanted to attract his attention to her. She had done it and he did not know it. Horrible. They were both caught in something. She had wanted to be caught, together with this agonising priestliness. But it was a trick. Perhaps they hated each other now.

"It is jolly to talk about things," she said, as the blood surged into her face.

He was grave again and did not answer.

"People don't talk about things nearly enough," she pursued.

10

"I saw Miriam through the window, *deep* in conversation with a most interesting young man."

"Have those people written about the bouquets?" said Miriam irritably.... Then mother had moved about the new house and was looking through those drawing-room windows this afternoon. She had looked about the house with someone else, saying all the wrong things, admiring things in the wrong way, impressed in the wrong way, having no thoughts, and no one with her to tell her what to think....

She flashed a passionate glance towards the clear weak flexible voice, half seeing the flushed face ... you're not upset about the weddings— "Miriam's scandalous goings-on the whole day long," said somebody ... because you've got me. You don't know me. You wouldn't like me if you did. You don't know him. He doesn't know you. But I know you, that's the difference....

"I've just thought something out," she said aloud, her voice drowned by two or three voices and the sound of things being served and handed about the supper-table. They were trying to draw her—still talking about the young men and her "goings-on." They did not know how far away she was and how secure she felt. She laughed towards her mother and smiled at her until she made her blush. Ah, she thought proudly, it's I who am your husband. Why have I not been with you all your life?... all the times you were alone; I knew them all. No one else knows them.

"I say," she insisted, "what about the bouquets?"

Mrs. Henderson raised her eyebrows helplessly and smiled, disclaiming.

"Hasn't anybody done anything?" roared Miriam.

Mary came in with a dish of fruit. Everyone went on so placidly.... She thought of the perfect set of her white silk bridesmaid's dress, its freshness, its clear apple green pipings, the little green leaves and fresh pink cluster roses on the white chip hat. If the shower bouquets did not come it would be simply ghastly. And everybody went on chattering.

She leaned anxiously across the table to Harriett.

"Oo—what's up?" asked Harriett.

Conversation had dropped. Miriam sat up to fling out her grievances.

"Well—just this. I'm told Gerald said the people would send a line to say it was all right, and they haven't written, and so far as I can make out nothing's been done."

"Bouquets would appear to be one of the essentials of the ceremony," hooted Mr. Henderson.

"Well, of course," retorted Miriam savagely, "if you *have* a dress wedding at all. That's the point."

"Quite so, my dear, quite so. I was unaware that you were depending on a message."

"I'm not anxious. It's simply silly, that's all."

"It'll be all right," suggested Harriett, looking into space. "They'd have written."

"Well, it's your old bouquet principally."

"Me. With a bouquet. Hoo——"

11

"Peace I give unto you, My peace I give unto you. Not as the world giveth, give I unto you——"

Christ said that. But peace came from God—the peace of God that passeth all understanding. How could Christ give that? He put Himself between God and man. Why could not people get at God direct? He was somewhere.

The steam was disappearing out of the window; the row of objects ranged along the far side of the bath grew clear. Miriam looked at them, seeking escape from the problem—the upright hand-glass, the brush bag propped against it, the small bottle of Jockey Club, the little pink box of French face powder ... perhaps one day she would learn to use powder without looking like a pierrot ... how nice to have a thick white skin that never changed and took powder like a soft bloom....

But as long as the powder box were there it would be impossible to reach that state of peace and freedom that Thomas à Kempis meant. "To Miriam, from her friend, Harriett A. Perne." Had Miss Haddie found anything of it? No—she was horribly afraid of God and turned to Christ as a sort of protecting lover to be flattered and to lean upon....

There were so many exquisite and wise things in the book; the language was so beautiful. But somehow there was a whining going all through it ... fretfulness. Anger too—"I had rather feel compunction than know the definition thereof." Why not both? He was talking at someone in that sentence.

The Kingdom of Heaven is *within* you. But even Christ went about sad, trying to get people to do some sort of trick that He said was necessary before they could find God—something to do with Himself. There was something wrong about that.

If one were perfectly still, the sense of God was there.

Supposing everyone could be got to stay perfectly still, until they died ... like that woman in the book who was dying so happily of starvation ... and then the friend came fussing in with soup....

Things were astounding enough; enough to make you die of astonishment, if you did nothing at all. Being *alive*. If one could realise that clearly enough, one *would* die.

Everything everyone did was just a distraction from astonishment.

It could only be done in a convent.... It cost money to get into a convent, except as a servant. If you were a servant you could not stay day and night in your cell—watching the light and darkness until you died.... Perhaps in women's convents they would not let you anyhow.

Why did men always have more freedom?... His head had a listening look. His eyes were waiting desperately, seeing nothing of the things in the world ... he wanted to stay still until the voice of things grew so clear and near that one could give a great cry and fall dead ... a long long cry.... Your hot heart, all of you, pouring out, getting free. Perhaps that happened to people when they were happy. They cried out to each other and were free— lost in another person. Whoso would save his soul ... but then they grew strange and apart.... Marriage was a sort of inferior condition ... an imitation of something else.... Ho-o-zan-na-in-the-Hi...i...est ... the top note rang up and stayed right up, in the rafters of the church.

"Did you ever notice how white the insides of your wrists are?"

Why did Bob seem so serious?... What a bother, what a bother.

It is a good thing to be plain ... "the tragedy of beauty; woman's greatest curse." ... Andromeda on a rock with her hair blowing over her face....

She was afraid to look at the monster coming out of the sea. If she had looked at it, it would not have dared to come near her. Because Perseus looked and rescued her, she would have to be grateful to him all her life and smile and be Mrs. Perseus. One day they would quarrel and he would never think her beautiful again....

Adam had not faced the devil. He was stupid first, and afterwards a coward and a cad ... "the divine curiosity of Eve...." Some person had said that.... Perhaps men would turn round one day and see, what they were like. Eve had not been unkind to the devil; only Adam and God. All the men in the world, and their God, ought to apologise to women....

To hold back and keep free ... and real. Impossible to be real unless you were quite free.... Two married in one family was enough. Eve would marry, too.

But money.

The chair-bed creaked as she knelt up and turned out the gas. "I love you" ... just a quiet manly voice ... perhaps one would forget everything, all the horrors and mysteries ... because there would be somewhere then always to be, to rest, and feel sure. If only ... just to sit hand in hand ... watching snowflakes ... to sit in the lamplight, quite quiet.

Pictures came in the darkness ... lamplit rooms, gardens, a presence, understanding.

12

Voices were sounding in the next room. Something being argued. A voice level and reassuring; going up now and again into a hateful amused falsetto. Miriam refused to listen. She had never been so near before. Of course they talked in their room. They had talked all their lives; an endless conversation; he laying down the law ... no end to it ... the movement of his beard as he spoke, the red lips shining through the fair moustache ... splash baths and no soap; soap is not a cleansing agent ... he had a ruddy skin ... healthy.

A tearful, uncertain voice....

"Don't mother ... don't, don't ... he can't understand.... Come to me! Come in here.... Well, well!..." A loud clear tone moving near the door, "Leave it all to nature, my dear...."

They're talking about Sally and Harriett.... He is *amused* ... like when he says "the marriage service begins with 'dearly beloved' and ends with 'amazement.' ..."

She turned about, straining away from the wall and burying her head in her pillow. Something seemed to shriek within her, throwing him off, destroying, flinging him away. Never again anything but contempt....

She lay weak and shivering in the uncomfortable little bed. Her heart was thudding in her throat and in her hands ... beloved ... beloved ... a voice, singing—

"So ear-ly *in* the mor-ning,

My beloved—my beloved."

Silence, darkness and silence.

13

Waking in the darkness, she heard the fluttering of leafage in the garden and lay still and cool listening and smiling. That went on ... flutter, flutter, in the breeze. It was enough ... and things happened, as well, in the far far off things called "days."

14

A fearful clamour—bright sunlight; something sticking sideways through the partly opened door—a tin trumpet. It disappeared with a flash as she leapt out of bed. The idea of Harriett being up first!

Harriett stood on the landing in petticoat and embroidered camisole, her hair neatly pinned, her face glowing and fresh.

"Gerrup," she said at once.

"You *up*. You oughtn't to be. I'm going to get your breakfast. You mustn't dress yourself...."

"Rot! You hurry up, old silly, breakfast's nearly ready."

She ran upstairs tootling her trumpet. "Hurry up," she said, from the top of the stairs, with a friendly grin.

Miriam shouted convivially and retired into her crowded sunlit bathroom, turning on both bath taps so that she might sing aloud. Harriett had made the day strong ... silver bright and clean and clear. Harriett was like a clear blade. She splashed into the cold water gasping and singing. Two o'clock—ages yet before the weddings. There was a smell of bacon frying. They would all have breakfast together. She could smile at Harriett. They had grown up together and could admit it, because Harriett was going away. But not for ages. She flew through her toilet; the little garden was blazing. It was a fine hot day.

15

Bennett and Gerald had turned strained pale faces to meet the brides as they came up the aisle. Now, Bennett's broad white forehead seemed to give out a radiance. It had been fearful to stand behind Harriett through the service listening to the bland hollow voice of the vicar and the four unfamiliar low voices responding, and taking the long glove smooth and warm from Harriett's hand, her rustling heavy-scented bouquet. At the sight of Bennett's grave radiant face the fear deepened and changed. Marriage was a reality ... fearful, searching reality; it changed people's expressions. Hard behind came Gerald and Harriett; Gerald's long face still pale, his loosely knit figure carried along by her tense little frame as she walked, a little firm straight figure of satin, her veil thrown back from her little snub face, her face held firmly; steady and old with its solid babyish curves and its brave stricken eyes: old and stricken; that was how Sarah had looked too. No radiance on the faces of Sarah and Harriett.

The Wedding March was pealing out from the chancel, a great tide of sound blaring down through the church and echoing back from the west window, near the door where they would all go out, in a moment, out into the world. On they went; how swift it all was.... Sarah and Harriett, rescued from poverty and fear ... mother's wedding on a May morning long ago ... in the little village church ... to walk out of church into the open country; in the morning; a bride. There were no brides in London.

Now to fall in behind Eve and Mr. Tremayne. Mr. Grove walked clumsily. His arm brushed against the shower bouquet.

The upturned faces of the pink carnations were fresh and sweet; for nothing. To-morrow they would be dead. Harriett's bouquet, dead too ... a wonderful dead bouquet that meant life. "Where are you, my friend, my own friend?"

16

A wedding seemed to make everybody happy. The people moving in Harriett's new rooms were happy. Old people were new and young. They laughed.... The sad dark man, following with his tray of glasses as she went from guest to guest with Harriett's champagne cup had laughed again and again....

The voices of the grey-clad bridegrooms rang about the rooms full of quiet relieved laughter. The outlines of their well-cut grey clothes were softly pencilled with a radiance of marriage. Round about Sarah and Eve was a great radiance. Light streamed from their satin dresses. But they were untouched. Silent and untouched and far away. What should these strange men ever know of them; coming and going?

17

She found herself standing elbow to elbow with Harriett. Warm currents came to her from Harriett's body; she moved her elbow against Harriett's to draw her attention. Harriett turned a scorched cheek and a dilated unseeing eye. Their hands dropped and met. Miriam felt the quivering of firm, strong fingers and the warm metal of rings. She grasped the matronly hand with the whole strength of her own. Harriett must remember ... all this wedding was nothing.... She was Harriett ... not the Mrs. Ducayne Bob Greville had just been talking to about Curtain Lectures and the Rascality of the Genus Homo ... she must remember all the years of being together, years of nights side by side ... night turning to day for both of them, at the same moment. She gave her hand a little shake. Harriett made a little skipping movement and grinned her own ironic grin. It was all right. They were quite alone and irreverent; they two; the festive crowd was playing a game for their amusement. They laughed without a sound as they had so often done in church. The air that encircled them was the air of their childhood.

18

Gerald's voice sounded near. It made no break in their union though Harriett welcomed it, clearing her throat with a businesslike cough.

"Time you changed, Mrs. La Reine," said Gerald, in a frightened friendly voice.

"Oh, lor, is it?" ... that kindliness was only in Harriett's voice when she had hurt someone.

... The edge of Gerald's voice, kind to everyone, would always be broken when he spoke to Harriett. She would always be this young absurd Harriett to him, always. He would go on fastening her boots for her tenderly, and go happily about his hobbies. She would never hear him call her "my dear." That old-fashioned mock-polite insolence of men ... paterfamilias.

19

The four of them were together in a room again, fastening and hooking and adjusting; standing about before mirrors. We've all grown up together ... we can admit it now ... we're admitting it. Everything clear, back to the beginning; happy and good. The room was still with the hush of its fresh draperies, hemming them in. Beautiful immortal forms moved in the room, reaping ... voices, steady and secure, said nothing but the necessary things, borne down with wealth, all the wealth there was ... all the laughter and certainty. Immortality. Nothing could die. They saw and knew everything. Each tone was a confession and a song of truth. They need never meet and speak again. They had known. The voices of Sarah and Harriett would go on ... marked with fresh things.... Her own and Eve's would remain, separate, to grow broken and false and unrecognisable in the awful struggle for money. No matter. The low secure untroubled tone of a woman's voice. There was nothing like it on earth.... If you had once heard it ... in your own voice, and the voice of another woman responding ... everything was there.

20

Was there anyone who fully realised how amazing it was ... a human tone. Perhaps everyone did, really, most people without knowing it. A few knew. Perhaps that was what kept life going.

21

In a few minutes they would go. They avoided each other's eyes. Miriam began to be afraid Eve would say something cheerful, or sing a snatch of song, desecrating the singing that was there, the deep eternal singing in each casual tone.

Gerald's whistle came up from the front garden.

Miriam opened the door. Bennett's voice came from the hall, calling for Sarah.

"Your skirt sets simply perfectly, Sally." ... Sarah was at the door in her neat soft dark blue travelling dress, and a soft blue straw hat with striped ribbon bands and bows, hurrying forward, her gold hair shining under her hat; seeing nothing but the open door downstairs and Bennett waiting.

22

The garden and pathway was thronged with bright-coloured guests. Miriam found herself standing with Gerald on the curb, waiting for Harriett to finish her farewells. He crushed her arm against his side. "Good Lord, Mirry, ain't I glad it's all over."

Sarah was stepping into the shelter of the first of the two waiting carriages. Her face was clear with relief. Bennett followed, dressed like her in dark blue. On the step he spoke abruptly, something about a small portmanteau. Sarah's voice sounded from inside. Miriam had never heard her speak with such cool unconcern. Perhaps she had never known Sarah. Sarah was herself now, for the first time free and unconcerned. What freedom. Cool and unconcerned. The door shut with a bang. They had forgotten everyone. They were going to forget to wave. Everyone had watched them. But they did not think of that. They saw green Devonshire ahead and their little house waiting in the Upper Richmond Road with work for them both, work they could both do well, with all their might when they came back. Someone shouted. Rice was being showered. People were running down the road showering rice. The road and pathway were bright with happy marriage, all the world linked in happy marriages.

23

The second carriage swept round the bend of the road with a yellow silk slipper swinging in the rear. Miriam struggled for breath through tears. Gerald and Harriett had taken the old life away with them in their carriage. Harriett had taken it, and gone. But she knew. She would bring it back with her. They would come back. Harriett would never forget. Nothing could change or frighten her. She would come back the same, in her new dresses, laughing.

A fat voice ... Mrs. Bywater ... "proud of your gails, Mrs. Henderson" ... fat flattering voice. The brightness had gone from the houses and the roadway ... unreal people were moving about with absurd things on their heads. Bridesmaids in cold white dresses, moving in pounces, as people spoke to them ... the Hendon girls.... What bad complexions Harriett's school friends had. Why were they all dark? Why did Harriett like them? Who was Harriett? Why did she have dark, sallow friends? Oh ... this dark face, near and familiar ... saying something—eyes looking at nothing; haunted eyes looking at nothing, very dear and familiar ... relief ... the sky seems to lift again; kind harmless bitter features, coming near and speaking.

"I am obliged to go——" rasping voice, curious sawing breath....

"Oh yes...." Perhaps there will be a thunderstorm or something—something will happen.

"We shall meet again."

"Yes—oh, yes."

24

There was no reason to feel nervous, at any rate for a night or two. Burglars who wanted the presents would take some time to find out that there was only one young lady in the house and a little servant sleeping in a top room. It was all right. No need to put the dinner-bell on the dressing-table. Next week the middle-aged servant would have arrived. Would she mind being alone with the presents and the little maid? The only way to feel quite secure at night would be to marry ... how awful ... either you marry and are never alone or you risk being alone and afraid ... to marry for safety

... perhaps some women did. No wonder ... and not to turn into a silly scared nervous old maid ... how tiresome, one thing or the other ... no choice.

She laid her head on the pillow. Thank Heaven I'm here and not at home ... out of it.... "I'll come round, first thing, to cut up the cake"—that would be jolly too. But here ... with all these new things, magical and easy, secure with Gerald and Harriett, chosen to embark on their new life with them.... "You chuck your job, my dear, and stay with us for a bit." They would like it. That was so jolly. Absurd free days with Harriett; tea in the garden, theatres; people coming, Mr. Tremayne and Mr. Grove....

But there was something, some thought sweeping round all these things, something else, sweeping round outside the weddings and the joy of being at home, making all these things extra, like things thrown in, jolly and perfect and surprising, but thrown in with something else that was her own, something hovering around and above, in and out the whole day keeping her apart. This morning the weddings had seemed the end of everything. They were over, Harriett's and Sarah's lives going forward and her own share in them, and home still there too, three things instead of one, easily hers. And yet they did not concern her. It would be a sham to pretend they did, with this other thing haunting—to go on from thing to thing, living with people and for them as if there were nothing else, as people seemed to do, one thing happening after another all the time. Sham.

Harriett and Sarah had rushed out into life. They had changed everything. Things did not seem to matter now that they had achieved all that. Harriett would take the first shock of life for her. Curiosities could come to an end. It did not seem to matter. That was all at peace, through Harriett. Life had come into the family, leaving her free....

Was she free? That strange, dark priestliness. If he called to her, if he really called.... But he called in a dark dreadful way ... and yet mysteriously linked to something in her. She could not give the help he needed. She would fail. Over their lives would shine, far away, visible to both of them the radiance of heaven. They both wanted to be good; redemption from sin. They both believed these things. But he was weak, weak ... and she not strong enough to help. And there was that other thing beckoning far from this suburban life and quite as far from him, away, up in London, down at Newlands, a brightness....

She looked through the darkness at the harmony of soft tones and draperies at distant Newlands ... etchings; the strange effect of etchings ... there were no etchings in the suburbs ... curious, close, strong lines that rested you and had a meaning and expression even though you did not understand the subject. There were so many things to take you away from people. In the suburbs people were everything, and there was nothing in them. They did not understand anything; but going on. They were helpless and without thoughts; amongst their furniture. They did not even have busts of Beethoven. At Newlands people might be dead, the women in bright hard deaths or deaths of cold, cruel deceitfulness, the men tiny insects of selfishness, but there were things that made up for everything full and satisfying.

And Salviati's window....

She must hold on to these things. Life without them would be impossible.

It was—Style ... or something. Le style c'est l'homme. That meant something. It was the same with clothes.... Suburban people could be fashionable, never stylish. And manners.... They were fussily kind and nice to each other; as if life were pitiful ... *life* ... pitiful. They all pitied, and despised each other.

25

The night was vast with all the other things. No need to sleep. To lie happy and strong in the sense of them was better than sleep. In a few hours the little suburban day would come ... everything gleaming with the light of the big things beyond. One could go through it in a drowse of strength, full of laughter ... laughter to the brim, all one's limbs strong and heavy with laughter.

Bob Greville had gone jingling down the road in a hansom—grey holland blinds and a pink rosebud in the driver's buttonhole. Why had he come? Going in and out of the weddings a pale grey white-spatted guest, talking to everyone ... a preoccupied piece of the West End. Large club windows looking out on sunlit Piccadilly; a glimpse of the haze of the Green Park. Weddings must be laughable to him with his "Mrs. Caudle's Curtain Lectures" ideas. His wife was dead. She had been fearfully ill suddenly on their wedding tour ... at "Law*zanne*." That was the wrong way to pronounce Lausanne. And that wrong way of pronouncing was somehow part of his way of thinking about her. He seemed to remember nothing but her getting ill and spoke with a sort of laughing, contemptuous *fear*. Men.

But in some way he was connected with that strange thing outside the everyday things.

26

How stupid of Eve to be vexed because she was told there was no need to scrawl the addresses of the little cake boxes right across the labels. Impossible now to ask her to come and play song accompaniments. Besides, she was tired. Eve was tired because she did not really know how glorious life was. In her life with the Greens in Wiltshire there was nothing besides the Greens but the beautiful landscape. And the landscape seen from the Greens' windows must look commercial, in the end. Eve was evidently beginning to tire of it. And they had worked so hard all the morning cutting up the cake. Eve did not know that towards the end of the morning she had thought of singing after lunch ... feeling so strong and wanting to make a noise. Bohm's songs. It was better really to sing to one's own accompaniment; only there was no one to listen....

"Und wenn i dann mal wie-ie-d-er *komm*."

a German girl, her face *strahlend mit Freude—radiant* with joy ... but *strahlend* was more than radiant ... streaming—like sunlight—shafts of sunlight. German women were not self-conscious. They were full of joy and sorrow. Perhaps *happier* than any other women. Their mountains and woods and villages and towns were beautiful with joy. They did not care what men thought or said. They were happy in their beautiful country in their own way. Germany ... all washed with poetry and music and song. "Freue dich des Lebens." *Freue ... Freue dich* ... the words were like the rush of wings ... the flutter of a fresh skirt round happy hurrying feet.

27

"What a melancholy ditty, chick."

Miriam laughed and dropped into the accompaniment of Schubert's "Ave Maria." "Listen, mother ... there was a monk who sang this so beautifully in a church that he had to be stopped." She played through the "Ave Maria" and looked round. Mrs. Henderson was sitting stiffly in a stiff straight chair with her hands twisted in her lap. "Oh bother," thought Miriam, "she's feeling hysterical ... and it's my turn this time. What on earth shall I do?" The word had come up through the years. Sarah had seen "attacks of hysteria...." Was she going to have one now ... laugh and cry and say dreadful things and then be utterly exhausted? Good Lord, how fearful. And what was the good? She "couldn't help it." That was why you had to be firm with hysterical people. But there was no need, now. Everything was better. Two of them married; the boys ready to look after everything. It was simply irritating ... and the sun just coming round into the green of the conservatory....

She sat impatient, feeling young and strong and solid with joy on the piano stool. Couldn't mother see her, sitting there in a sort of blaze of happy strength? She swung impatiently round to the keyboard and glanced at the open album. There was silence in the room. Her heart beat anxiously ... some

German printer had printed those notes ... in pain and illness perhaps—but pain and illness in *Germany*, not in this dreadful little room where despair was shut in.... "Comus," "The Seven Ages of Man," "The Arctic Regions," beautiful bindings on the little old inlaid table, things belonging to those sunny beginnings and ending with that awful agonised figure sitting there silent. She cleared her throat and stretched a hand out over the notes of a chord without striking it. Something was gaining on her. Something awful and horrible.

"Play something cheerful, chickie," said her mother, in a dreadful deep trembling voice. Suddenly Miriam knew, in horror, that the voice wanted to scream, to bellow. Bellow ... that huge, tall woman striding about on the common at Worthing ... bellowing ... mad—madness. She summoned, desperately, something in herself, and played a thing she disliked, wondering why she chose it. Her hands played carefully, holding to the rhythm, carefully avoiding pressure and emphasis. Nothing could happen as long as she could keep on playing like that. It made the music seem like a third person in the room. It was a new way of playing. She would try it again when she was alone. It made the piece wonderful ... traceries of tone shaping themselves one after another, intertwining, and stopping against the air ... tendrils on a sunlit wall.... She had a clear conviction of manhood ... that strange hard feeling that was always twining between her and the things people wanted her to do and to be. Manhood with something behind it that understood. This time it was welcome. It served. She asserted it, sadly feeling it mould the lines of her face.

28

The end of the piece was swift and tuneful and stormy, the only part she had cared for hitherto. For a moment she was tempted to dash into it ... her hands were so able and strong, so near to mastery of the piano after that curious careful playing. But it would be cruel. She passed on to the final chords—broad and even and simple. They suggested quiet music going on, playing itself in the room. Getting up beaming and shy and embarrassed she did not dare to look at the waiting figure, and looked busily into the dark interiors of the bowls and vases along the mantelpiece.... There was something in the waiting figure that did not want to scream. Something exactly like herself.... At the bottom of one of the deep bowls was a curling-pin. She giggled, catching her breath.

Mrs. Henderson glanced up at her and looked away, looking about the room. That's naughty, thought Miriam. She's not trying; she's being naughty and tiresome. Perhaps she's angry with me, and thinks I mean she must just go on enduring.

"I can't correct a misprint with a curling-pin."

Mother believed in the misprint.... Talk on about misprints ... why was it necessary to be insincere if one wanted to make anything happen? But anything was better than saying, What is the matter? That would be just as insincere, and impudent too.

"These cheap things are always so badly printed."

"Oh!" ... Mother's polite tone, trying to be interested. That was all she'd had for years. All she'd ever had, from him. Miriam sat down conversationally, in a long chair. She felt a numb sleepiness coming over her, and stretched all her muscles lazily, to their full limit ... mother, just mother in the room, perfect ease and security ... and relaxed with a long yawn, feeling serenely awake. The little figure ceased to be horrible.

"My life has been so useless," said Mrs. Henderson suddenly.

Here it was ... a jolt ... an awful physical shock, jarring her body.... She braced herself and spoke quickly and blindly ... a network of feeling vibrated all over to and fro, painfully.

"It only seems so to you," she said, in a voice muffled by the beating of her heart. Anything might happen—she had no power.... Mother—almost killed by things she could not control, having done her duty all her life ... doing thing after thing had not satisfied her ... being happy and brave had not satisfied her. There was something she had always wanted, for herself ... even mother....

Mrs. Henderson shuddered and sighed. Her pose relaxed a little.

"I might have done something for the poor."

"Oh, yes? What things?" She had lived in a nightmare of ways and means, helpless....

"I might have made clothes, sometimes...."

"That worries you, so that you can hardly bear it."

"Yes."

"It needn't. I don't mean the poor need not be helped. But you needn't have that feeling."

"You understand it?"

"I feel it this moment, as you feel it."

"Well?"

"You needn't."

Miriam held back her thoughts. Nothing mattered but to sit there holding back thought and feeling and argument, if only she could without getting angry.... There was something here, something decisive. This was what she had been born for, if only she could hold on. She felt very old. No more happiness ... the little house they sat in was a mockery, a fiendish contrivance to hide agony. There was nothing in these little houses in themselves, just indifference hiding miseries.

She sat forward conversationally. A rain of tears was coming down her companion's cheeks. To hold on ... hold on ... not to think or feel glad or sorry ... it would be impudent to feel anything ... to hold on if the tears went on for an hour ... treating them as if they were part of a conversation.

"You understand me?"

"Of course."

"You are the only one."

The relieved voice ... steady, as she had known it correcting her in her babyhood.

"I should be better if I could be more with you ..." oh Lord ... impossible.

"You must be with me as much as you like."

That was the thing. That was what must be done somehow.

"Mother! would you mind if I smoked a cigarette?"

It was suddenly possible, the unheard-of unconfessed ... suddenly easy and possible.

"My dearest child!" Mrs. Henderson's flushed face crimsoned unresistingly. She was shocked and ashamed and half delighted. Miriam gazed boldly, admiring and adoring. She felt she had embarked on her first real flirtation and blessed the impulse that had that morning transferred cigarettes and matches from her handbag to her hanging pocket as a protection against suburban influence and a foretaste of her appointment with Bob. She lit a cigarette with downcast lids and a wicked smile, throwing a triumphant possessive glance at her mother as it drew. The cigarette was divine. It was divine to smoke like this, countenanced and beloved— scandalous and beloved.

29

Miriam ran all the way to the station. The gardens on either side of Gipsy Lane were full of flowering shrubs massed up against laburnum and May trees in flower ... fresh clean colours, pink and lilac and yellow and everywhere new bright fresh green ... May. She flung herself into an empty carriage of the three o'clock Vauxhall and Waterloo train, her eyes filled with the maze of garden freshness and was carried off along the edge of the common, streaming blazing green in the full sunlight, dotted with gorse. Bob would not have to wait at Waterloo.... Further down the line, towards Kew, was the mile of orchards, close on either side of the line, thick with bloom.... Walls and houses began to appear. She took her eyes from the window and the gardens and the common and the imagined orchards passed before her eyes in the dusty enclosure. As she gazed they seemed to pass through her, the freshness of the blossoms backed by fresh greenery was a feeling, cool and fresh in her blood. The growing intensity of this feeling stirred her to movement and consciousness of the dust-filmed carriage, the smell of dust. Still again, the sight of the spring flowing from her eyes, into them, out through them, breathing with her breath, the feeling of spring in the soft beating from head to foot of her blood, was all there was anywhere out to the limits of space. The dusty carriage was a speck in the great fresh tide, and the vision of Eve drifting in the carriage, in the corner, opposite, with pale frightened face, saying the things she had said just now, was no longer terrifying, though each thing she said came clearly, a separate digging blow.

... "Dr. Ryman is giving her bromide ... she can't sleep without it." Sleeplessness, insomnia ... she can't see the spring ... why not; and forget about herself.

"It's nerves. He says we must behave as if there was nothing wrong with her. There *is* nothing wrong but nerves."

That fevered frame, the burning hands and burning eyes looking at everything in the wrong way, the brain seeking about, thinking first this and then that ... nerves; and fat Dr. Ryman giving bromide ... awful little bottles of bromide coming to the house wrapped up in white paper. And everyone satisfied. "She's in Dr. Ryman's hands. Dr. Ryman is treating her." Mrs. Poole said Dr. Ryman was a very able man. What did she mean? How did she know? Suburban faces; satisfied. "In the doctor's hands." A large square house, a square garden, high walls, a delicate wife always being ill, always going to that place in Germany—how did he know, going about in a brougham—and he had gout ... how did he know more than anyone else? ... bottles of bromide, visits, bills, and mother going patiently on, trusting and feeling unhelped. Going on. People went ... mad. If she could not sleep she would go ... *mad*.... And everyone behaving as if nothing were wrong.

And the vicar! Praying in the dining-room. Sarah had heard.... The vicar, kneeling on the Turkey carpet ... praying. Couldn't God see her, on the carpet, praying and trying? And the vicar went away. And things were the same and that night she would not sleep, just the same. Of course not.

Nothing was changed. It was all going on for her in some hot wrong, shut-up way. Bromide and prayers.

30

And she blamed herself. If only she would not blame herself. "He's one in a thousand ... if only I could be as calm and cool as he is." Why not be calm and cool? She had gone too far ... "the end of my tether" ... mother, a clever phrase like that, where had she got it? It was true. Her suffering had taught her to find that awful phrase. She feared her room, "loathed" it. She, always gently scolding exaggeration, used and meant that violent word.

31

Money. That was why nothing had been done. "The doctor" had to be afforded as she was so ill, but nothing had been done. Borrow from the boys to take her away. "A bright place and a cool breeze." She dreamed of things—far-away impossible things. Had she told the others she wanted them? They must be told. To-morrow she should know she was going away. Nothing else in life mattered. Someone must pay, anyone. Newlands must go. To-morrow and every day till they went away she should come round to Harriett's new house. Something for her to do every day.

The little bonneted figure ... happy, shocked, smiling. To go about with her, telling her everything, dreadful things. The two of them going about and talking and not talking, and going about.

32

Miriam moved uneasily to the mantelpiece. An unlit fire was laid neatly in the grate. A ray of sunlight struck the black bars of the grate; false uneasy sunlight. Two strange round-bowled long-necked vases stood on the mantelpiece amongst the litter of Bob's belongings. Dull blue and green enamellings moving on a dark almost black background ... strange fine little threads of gold.... She peered at them.

"My dear girl, do you like my vases?" Bob came and stood at her side.

"Yes—they're funny and queer. I like them."

"They're clawzonny—Japanese clawzonny." He took one of them up and tapped it with his nail. It gave out a curious dull metallic ring. Miriam passed her finger over the enamelled surface. It was softly smooth and with no chill about it; as if the enamel were alive. She marvelled at the workmanship, wondering how the gold wires were introduced. They gleamed, veining over the curves of the vase.

Her uneasiness had gone. While they were looking at the vases it did not seem to matter that she had consented, defying the whole world, to come and see Bob's bachelor chambers. She did not like them and wanted to be gone. The curious dingy dustiness oppressed her, and there was an emptiness. Fancy having breakfast in a room like this. Who looked after a man's washing when he lived alone? There must be some dreadful sort of charwoman who came, and Bob had to speak kindly to her in his weary old voice and go on day after day being here. But the vases stood there alive and beautiful and he liked them. She turned to see his liking in his face. As she turned his arm came round her shoulders and the angle of his shoulder softly touched her head. Behind her head there was a point of perfect rest; comfort, perfect. Australia; a young man in shirt-sleeves, toiling and dreaming. Was that there still in his face?

"Are you happy, dear girl? Do you like being with old Bob in his den?"

He came nearer and spoke with a soft husky whisper.

"Let me go," said Miriam wearily, longing to rest, longing for the stairs they had come up and the open street in the sunshine and freedom.

She moved away and gathered up her gloves and scarf.

CHAPTER XI

1

Miriam sat with her mother near the bandstand. They faced the length of the esplanade with the row of houses that held their lodging to their right and the sea away to the left. She had found that it was better to sit facing a moving vista; forms passing by too near to be looked at and people moving in the distance too far away to suggest anything. The bandstand had filled. The town-clock struck eleven. Presently the band would begin to play. Any minute now. It had begun. The introduction to its dreamiest waltz was murmuring in a conversational undertone. The stare of the esplanade rippled and broke. The idling visitors became vivid blottings. The house-rows stood out in lines and angles. The short solemn symphony was over. Full and soft and ripe the euphonium began the beat of the waltz. It beat gently within the wooden kiosk. The fluted melody went out across the sea. The sparkling ripples rocked gently against the melody. A rousing theme would have been more welcome to the suffering at her side. She waited for the loud gay jerky tripping of the second movement. When it crashed brassily out the scene grew vivid. The air seemed to move; freshness of air and sea coming from the busy noise of the kiosk. The restless fingers ceased straying and plucking. The suffering had shifted. The night was over. When the waltz was over they would be able to talk a little. There would be something ... a goat-chaise; a pug with a solemn injured face. Until the waltz came to an end she turned towards the sea, wandering out over the gleaming ripples, hearing their soft sound, snuffing freshness, seeing the water just below her eyes, transparent green and blue and mauve, salt-filmed.

2

The big old woman's voice grated on about Poole's Miriorama. She had been a seven-mile walk before lunch and meant to go to Poole's Miriorama. She knew everything there was in it and went to it every summer and for long walks and washed lace in her room and borrowed an iron from Miss Meldrum. No one listened and her deep voice drowned all the sounds at the table. She only stopped at the beginning of a mouthful or to clear her throat with a long harsh grating sound. She did not know that there was nothing wonderful about Poole's Miriorama or about walking every morning to the end of the parade and back. She did not know that there were wonderful things. She was like her father ... she was mad. Miss Meldrum listened and answered without attending. The other people sat politely round the table and passed things with a great deal of stiff politeness. One or two of them talked suddenly, with raised voices. The others exclaimed. They were all in agreement ... "a young woman with a baritone voice" ... a frog, white, keeping alive in coal for hundreds of years ... my cousin has crossed the Atlantic six times.... Nothing of any kind would ever stop them. They would never wait to know they were alive. They were mad. They would die mad. Of diseases with names. Even Miss Meldrum did not quite know. When she talked she was as mad as they were. When she was alone in her room and not thinking about ways and means she read books of devotion and cried. If she had had a home and a family she would have urged her sons and daughters to get on and beat other people.... But she knew mother was different. All of them knew it in some way. They spoke to her now and again with deference, their faces flickering with beauty. They knew she was beautiful. Sunny and sweet and good, sitting there in her faded dress, her face shining with exhaustion.

3

They walked down the length of the pier through the stiff breeze arm in arm. The pavilion was gaslit, ready for the entertainment.

"Would you rather stay outside this afternoon?"

"No. Perhaps the entertainment may cheer me."

There was a pink paper with their tickets—"The South Coast Entertainment Company" ... that was better than the usual concert. The inside of the pavilion was like the lunch table ... the same people. But there was a yellow curtain across the platform. Mother could look at that. It was quite near them. It would take off the effect of the audience of people she envied. The cool sound of the waves flumping and washing against the pier came in through the open doors with a hollow echo. They were settled and safe for the afternoon. For two hours there would be nothing but the things behind the curtain. Then there would be tea. Mother had felt the yellow curtain. She was holding the pink programme at a distance trying to read it. Miriam glanced. The sight of the cheap black printing on the thin pink paper threatened the spell of the yellow curtain. She must manage to avoid reading it. She crossed her knees and stared at the curtain, yawning and scolding with an affected manliness about the forgotten spectacles. They squabbled and laughed. The flump-wash of the waves had a cheerful sunlit sound. Mrs. Henderson made a brisk little movement of settling herself to attend. The doors were being closed. The sound of the waves was muffled. They were beating and washing outside in the sunlight. The gaslit interior was a pier pavilion. It was like the inside of a bathing-machine, gloomy, cool, sodden with sea-damp, a happy caravan. Outside was the blaze of the open day, pale and blinding. When they went out into it it would be a bright unlimited jewel, getting brighter and brighter, all its colours fresher and deeper until it turned to clear deep live opal and softened down and down to darkness dotted with little pinlike jewellings of light along the esplanade; the dark luminous waves washing against the black beach until dawn.... The curtain was drawing away from a spring scene ... the fresh green of trees feathered up into a blue sky. There were boughs of apple-blossom. Bright green grass sprouted along the edge of a pathway. A woman floundered in from the side in a pink silk evening dress. She stood in the centre of the scene preparing to sing, rearing her gold-wigged head and smiling at the audience. Perhaps the players were not ready. It was a solo. She would get through it and then the play would begin. She smiled promisingly. She had bright large teeth and the kind of mouth that would say chahld for child. The orchestra played a few bars. She took a deep breath. "Bring back—the yahs—that are—dead!"—she screamed violently.

She was followed by two men in shabby tennis flannels with little hard glazed tarpaulin hats who asked each other riddles. Their jerky broken voices fell into cold space and echoed about the shabby pavilion. The scattered audience sat silent and still, listening for the voices ... cabmen wrangling in a gutter. The green scene stared stiffly—harsh cardboard, thin harsh paint. The imagined scene moving and flowing in front of it was going on somewhere out in the world. The muffled waves sounded near and clear. The sunlight was dancing on them. When the men had scrambled away and the applause had died down, the sound of the waves brought dancing gliding figures across the stage, waving balancing arms and unconscious feet gliding and dreaming. A man was standing in the middle of the platform with a roll of music—bald-headed and grave and important. The orchestra played the overture to "The Harbour Bar." But whilst he unrolled his music and cleared his throat his angry voice filled the pavilion: "it's all your own fault ... you get talking and gossiping and filling yer head with a lot of nonsense ... now you needn't begin it all over again twisting and turning everything I say." And no sound in the room but the sound of eating. His singing was pompous anger, appetite. Shame shone from his rim of hair. He was ashamed, but did not know that he showed it.

4

They could always walk home along the smooth grey warm esplanade to tea in an easy silence. The light blossoming from the horizon behind them was enough. Everything ahead dreamed in it, at peace. Visitors were streaming homewards along the parade lit like flowers. Along the edge of the tide the town children were paddling and shouting. After tea they would come out into the sheltering twilight at peace, and stroll up and down until it was time to go to the flying performance of The Pawnbroker's Daughter.

5

They were late for tea and had it by themselves at a table in the window of the little smoking-room looking out on the garden. Miss Meldrum called cheerily down through the house to tell them when they came in. They went into the little unknown room and the cook brought up a small silver tea-pot and a bright cosy. Outside was the stretch of lawn where the group had been taken in the morning a year ago. It had been a seaside town lawn, shabby and brown, with the town behind it; unnoticed because the fresh open sea and sky were waiting on the other side of the house ... seaside town gardens were not gardens ... the small squares of greenery were helpless against the bright sea ... and even against shabby rooms, when the sun came into the rooms off the sea ... sea-rooms.... The little smoking-room was screened by the shade of a tree against whose solid trunk half of the French window was thrown back.

When the cook shut the door of the little room the house disappeared. The front rooms bathed in bright light and hot with the afternoon heat, the wide afterglow along the front, the vast open lid of the sky, were in another world.... Miriam pushed back the other half of the window and they sat down in a green twilight on the edge of the garden. If others had been there Mrs. Henderson would have remarked on the pleasantness of the situation and tried to respond to it and been dreadfully downcast at her failure and brave. Miriam held her breath as they settled themselves. No remark came. The secret was safe. When she lifted the cosy the little tea-pot shone silver-white in the strange light. A thick grey screen of sky must be there, above the trees, for the garden was an intensity of deep brilliance, deep bright green and calceolarias and geraniums and lobelias, shining in a brilliant gloom. It was not a seaside garden ... it was a garden ... all gardens. They took their meal quietly and slowly, speaking in low tones. The silent motionless brilliance was a guest at their feast. The meal-time, so terrible in the hopelessness of home, such an effort in the mocking glare of the boarding-house was a great adventure. Mrs. Henderson ate almost half as much as Miriam, serenely. Miriam felt that a new world might be opening.

6

"The storm has cleared the air wonderfully."

"Yes; isn't it a blessing."

"Perhaps I shan't want the beef-tea to-night." Miriam hung up her dress in the cupboard, listening to the serene tone. The dreadful candle was flickering in the night-filled room, but mother was quietly making a supreme effort.

"I don't expect you will"; she said casually from the cupboard, "it's ready if you should want it. But you won't want it."

"It *is* jolly and fresh," she said a moment later from the window, holding back the blind. Perhaps in a few days it would be the real jolly seaside and she would be young again, staying there alone with mother, just ridiculous and absurd and frantically happy, mother getting better and better, turning into the fat happy little thing she ought to be, and they would get to know people and mother would have to look after her and love her high spirits and admire and scold her and be shocked as she used to be. They might even bathe. It would be heavenly to be really at the seaside with just mother. They would be idiotic.

Mrs. Henderson lay very still as Miriam painted the acid above the unseen nerve centres and composed herself afterwards quietly without speaking. The air was fresh in the room. The fumes of the acid did not seem so dreadful to-night.

The Pawnbroker's daughter was with them in the room, cheering them. The gay young man had found out somehow through her that "goodness and truth" were the heart of his life. She had not told him. It was he who had found it out. He had found the words and she did not want him to say them. But it was a new life for them both, a new life for him and happiness for her even if he did not come back, if she could forget the words.

Putting out the candle at her bedside suddenly and quietly with the match-box to avoid the dreadful puff that would tell her mother of night, Miriam lay down. The extinguished light splintered in the darkness before her eyes. The room seemed suddenly hot. Her limbs ached, her nerves blazed with fatigue. She had never felt this kind of tiredness before. She lay still in the darkness with open eyes. Mrs. Henderson was breathing quietly as if in a heavy sleep. She was not asleep but she was trying to sleep. Miriam lay watching the pawnbroker's daughter in the little room at the back of the shop, in the shop, back again in the little room, coming and going. There was a shining on her face and on her hair. Miriam watched until she fell asleep.

7

She dreamed she was in the small music-room in the old Putney school, hovering invisible. Lilla was practising alone at the piano. Sounds of the girls playing rounders came up from the garden. Lilla was sitting in her brown merino dress, her black curls shut down like a little cowl over her head and neck. Her bent profile was stern and manly, her eyes and her bare white forehead manly and unconscious. Her lissome brown hands played steadily and vigorously. Miriam listened incredulous at the certainty with which she played out her sadness and her belief. It shocked her that Lilla should know so deeply and express her lonely knowledge so ardently. Her gold-flecked brown eyes that commonly laughed at everything, except the problem of free-will, and refused questions, had as much sorrow and certainty as she had herself. She and Lilla were one person, the same person. Deep down in everyone was sorrow and certainty. A faint resentment filled her. She turned away to go down into the garden. The scene slid into the large music-room. It was full of seated forms. Lilla was at the piano, her foot on the low pedal, her hands raised for a crashing chord. They came down, collapsing faintly on a blur of wrong notes. Miriam rejoiced in her heart. What a fiend I am ... what a fiend, she murmured, her heart hammering condemnation. Someone was sighing harshly; to be heard; in the darkness; not far off; fully conscious she glanced at the blind. It was dark. The moon was not round. It was about midnight. Her face and eyes felt thick with sleep. The air was rich with sleep. Her body was heavy with a richness of sleep and fatigue. In a moment she could be gone again.... "Shall I get the beef-tea, mother?" ... she heard herself say in a thin wideawake voice. "Oh no my dear," sounded another voice patiently. Rearing her numb consciousness against a delicious tide of oncoming sleep she threw off the bed-clothes and stumbled to the floor. "You can't go on like this night after night, my dear." "Yes I can," said Miriam in a tremulous faint tone. The sleepless even voice reverberated again in the unbroken sleeplessness of the room. "It's no use ... I am cumbering the ground." The words struck sending a heat of anger and resentment through Miriam's shivering form. She spoke sharply, groping for the matches.

8

Hurrying across the cold stone floor of the kitchen she lit the gas from her candle. Beetles ran away into corners, crackling sickeningly under the fender. A mouse darted along the dresser. She braced herself to the sight of the familiar saucepan, Miss Meldrum's good beef-tea brown against the white enamel—helpless ... waiting for the beef-tea to get hot she ate a biscuit. There was help somewhere. All those people sleeping quietly upstairs. If she asked them to they would be surprised and kind. They would suggest rousing her and getting her to make efforts. They would speak in rallying voices, like Dr. Ryman and Mrs. Skrine. For a day or two it would be better and then much worse and she would have to go away. Where? It would be the same everywhere. There was no one in the world who could help. There was something ... if she could leave off worrying. But that had been Pater's advice all his life and it had not helped. It was something more than leaving off ... it was something real. It was not affection and sympathy. Eve gave them; so easily, but they were not big enough. They did not come near enough. There was something crafty and worldly about them. They made a sort of prison. There was something true and real somewhere. Mother knew it. She had learned how useless even the good kind people were and was alone, battling to get at something. If only she could get at it and rest in it. It was there, everywhere. It was here in the kitchen, in the steam rising from the hot beef-tea. A moon-ray came through the barred window as she turned down the gas. It was clear in the eye of the moon-ray; a real thing.

Some instinct led away from the New Testament. It seemed impossible to-night. Without consulting her listener Miriam read a psalm. Mrs. Henderson put down her cup and asked her to read it again. She read and fluttered pages quietly to tell the listener that in a moment there would be some more. Mrs. Henderson waited saying nothing. She always sighed regretfully over the gospels and Saint Paul, though she asked for them and seemed to think she ought to read them. They were so dreadful; the gospels full of social incidents and reproachfulness. They seemed to reproach everyone and to hint at a secret that no one possessed ... the epistles did nothing but nag and threaten and probe. St. Paul rhapsodised sometimes ... but in a superior way ... patronising; as if no one but himself knew anything....

"How beautiful upon the mountains are the feet of those who bring" she read evenly and slowly. Mrs. Henderson sighed quietly.... "That's Isaiah mother.... Isaiah is a beautiful name." ... She read on. Something had shifted. There was something in the room.... If she could go droning on and on in an even tone it would be there more and more. She read on till the words flowed together and her droning voice was thick with sleep. The town clock struck two. A quiet voice from the other bed brought the reading to an end. Sleep was in the room now. She felt sure of it. She lay down leaving the candle alight and holding her eyes open. As long as the candle was alight the substance of her reading remained. When it was out there would be the challenge of silence again in the darkness ... perhaps not; perhaps it would still be there when the little hot point of light had gone. There was a soft sound somewhere ... the sea. The tide was up, washing softly. That would do. The sound of it would be clearer when the light was out ... drowsy, lazy, just moving, washing the edge of the beach ... cool, fresh. Leaning over she dabbed the candle noiselessly and sank back asleep before her head reached the pillow.

9

In the room yellow with daylight a voice was muttering rapidly, rapid words and chuckling laughter and stillness. Miriam grasped the bedclothes and lay rigid. Something in her fled out and away, refusing. But from end to end of the world there was no help against this. It was a truth; triumphing over everything. "*I* know," said a high clear voice. "*I* know ... I don't deceive myself" ... rapid low muttering and laughter.... It was a conversation. Somewhere within it was the answer. Nowhere else in the world. Forcing herself to be still she accepted the sounds, pitting herself against the sense of destruction. The sound of violent lurching brought her panic. There was something there that would strike. Hardly knowing what she did she pretended to wake with a long loud yawn. Her body shivered, bathed in perspiration. "What a lovely morning" she said dreamily, "what a perfect morning." Not daring to sit up she reached for her watch. Five o'clock. Three more hours before the day began. The other bed was still. "It's going to be a magnificent day" she murmured pretending to stretch and yawn again. A sigh reached her. The stillness went on and she lay for an hour tense and listening. Something must be done to-day. Someone else must know.... At the end of an hour a descending darkness took her suddenly. She woke from it to the sound of violent language, furniture being roughly moved, a swift angry splashing of water ... something breaking out, breaking through the confinements of this little furniture-filled room ... the best gentlest thing she knew in the world openly despairing at last.

10

The old homœopathist at the other end of the town talked quietly on ... the afternoon light shone on his long white hair ... the principle of health, God-given health, governing life. To be well one must trust in it absolutely. One must practise trusting in God every day.... The patient grew calm, quietly listening and accepting everything he said, agreeing again and again. Miriam sat wondering impatiently why they could not stay. Here in this quiet place with this quiet old man, the only place in the world where anyone had seemed partly to understand, mother might get better. He could help. He knew what the world was like and that nobody understood. He must know that he ought to keep her. But he did not seem to want to do anything but advise them and send them away. She hated him, his serene white-haired pink-faced old age. He told them he was seventy-nine and had never taken a dose in his life. Leaving his patient to sip a glass of water into which he had measured drops of tincture he took Miriam to look at the greenhouse behind his consulting room. As soon as they were alone he told her speaking quickly and without benevolence and in the voice of a younger man that she must summon help, a trained attendant. There ought to be someone for night and day. He seemed to know exactly the way in which she had been taxed and spoke of her youth. It is very wrong for you to be alone with her he added gravely.

Vaguely, burning with shame at the confession she explained that it could not be afforded. He listened attentively and repeated that it was absolutely necessary. She felt angrily for words to explain the uselessness of attendants. She was sure he must know this and wanted to demand that he should help, then and there at once, with his quiet house and his knowledge. Her eye covered him. He was only a pious old man with artificial teeth making him speak with a sort of sibilant woolliness. Perhaps he too knew that in the end even this would fail. He made her promise to write for help and refused a fee. She hesitated helplessly, feeling the burden settle. He indicated that he had said his say and they went back.

On the way home they talked of the old man. "He is right; but it is too late" said Mrs. Henderson with clear quiet bitterness, "God has deserted me." They walked on, tiny figures in a world of huge grey-stone houses. "He will not let me sleep. He does not want me to sleep.... He does not care."

A thought touched Miriam, touched and flashed. She grasped at it to hold and speak it, but it passed off into the world of grey houses. Her cheeks felt hollow, her feet heavy. She summoned her strength, but her body seemed outside her, empty, pacing forward in a world full of perfect unanswering silence.

11

The bony old woman held Miriam clasped closely in her arms. "You must never, as long as you live, blame yourself my gurl." She went away. Miriam had not heard her come in. The pressure of her arms and her huge body came from far away. Miriam clasped her hands together. She could not feel them. Perhaps she had dreamed that the old woman had come in and said that. Everything was dream; the world. I shall not have any life. I can never have any life; all my days. There were cold tears running into her mouth. They had no salt. Cold water. They stopped. Moving her body with slow difficulty against the unsupporting air she looked slowly about. It was so difficult to move. Everything was airy and transparent. Her heavy hot light impalpable body was the only solid thing in the world, weighing tons; and like a lifeless feather. There was a tray of plates of fish and fruit on the table. She looked at it, heaving with sickness and looking at it. I am hungry. Sitting down near it she tried to pull the tray. It would not move. I must eat the food. Go on eating food, till the end of my life. Plates of food like these plates of food.... I am in eternity ... where their worm dieth not and their fire is not quenched.